THE DUSK COUNTRY

ALSO BY W. MICHAEL GEAR AND KATHLEEN O'NEAL GEAR

Big Horn Legacy

Dark Inheritance

The Foundation

Fracture Event

Long Ride Home

The Mourning War

Raising Abel

Rebel Hearts Anthology

Sand in the Wind

Thin Moon and Cold Mist

Black Falcon Nation Series

Flight of the Hawk Series

The Moundville Duology

Saga of a Mountain Sage Series

The Wyoming Chronicles

The Anasazi Mysteries

"Sure to keep readers turning the pages... As usual, the Gears, husband-and-wife archaeologists, have enriched and enhanced the gripping plot with plenty of anthropological, archaeological, and historical detail."

— *BOOKLIST*

THE DUSK COUNTRY

THE PEACEMAKER'S TALE
BOOK FOUR

W. MICHAEL GEAR

KATHLEEN O'NEAL GEAR

WOLFPACK
PUBLISHING
— EST 2010 —

The Dusk Country
Paperback Edition
Copyright © 2024 (As Revised) W. Michael Gear and
Kathleen O'Neal Gear

Wolfpack Publishing
701 S. Howard Ave. 106-324
Tampa, Florida 33609

wolfpackpublishing.com

Illustrations by Ellisa Mitchel.

Paperback ISBN 978-1-63977-175-2
eBook ISBN 978-1-63977-174-5

*To Mike D. O'Neal in memory of the lost years
when we didn't get to see each other.
It's great to have you back in this world.*

NONFICTION
INTRODUCTION

As those of you who read the introduction for *People of the Longhouse* know, during the thirteenth and fourteenth centuries, the size of Iroquois villages began to grow. Archaeologists call this "population aggregation," meaning that more and more people were crowding together within the palisaded walls of villages. We see these expanded longhouses at places like the Furnace Brook and Howlett Hill sites in New York, where archaeologists excavated houses that were 210 and 334 feet long. This Middle Iroquoian period also saw the people becoming increasingly dependent upon maize-bean-squash agriculture. As in historic times, men cleared the fields, built the houses, and hunted, while women were the farmers. They cultivated the soil, planted, tended the fields, harvested and stored the crops. When women began to account for more and more of the food, their lineages also probably became the dominant social avenue for prestige.

At around AD 1400, the first evidence for individual tribes appears. Differences in pottery styles, burial customs, and types of houses demonstrate divisions between Iroquoian groups. As well, small villages began to amalgamate with larger ones, forming cohesive social groups, or, we suspect, nations.

AD 1400 is also the time when the Iroquois were building the most impressive longhouses, and many were elaborately fortified. At the Schoff site outside of Onondaga, New York, the people constructed a longhouse 400 feet long, twenty-two feet wide, and nearly as tall. The palisaded settlement may have housed 1,500 to 2,000 people, consisting of many different clans.

For archaeologists, this type of aggregation is a telltale sign of interpersonal violence. Simply put, people crowd together for defensive purposes. Cannibalism also first appears in the Iroquoian archaeological record at this point, in the form of cut and cooked human bones.

The Dusk Country takes place at this critical moment in time.

Why did warfare break out? The fact that the climate had grown cooler and drier certainly contributed to the violence. We know that droughts were more frequent, growing seasons shorter, and we can tell from the skeletal remains that food shortages were more common. Larger villages deplete resources at a faster rate. Game populations, nut forests, firewood, and fertile soils would all have played out more quickly, which means the Iroquois must have had to move their villages more often. Moving may have brought them into conflict with neighbors just as desperate for the food resources.

At the Alhart site in the Oak Orchard Creek drainage in western New York, archaeologists found evidence of burned longhouses and food, and the dismembered remains of seventeen people —most of them male. Historically, it was common practice for women and children to either be killed on site, or taken captive and marched away while the male warriors were tortured to death. The fragments of a child's skull were found in one storage pit at the Alhart site, and the skull of a woman in another storage pit. As well, fifteen male skulls were found in a storage pit on top of charred corn, and were probably placed there as severed heads, in the flesh. Some of them were burned. Two had suffered blows to the front of the head. These are just a few examples of warfare. For more detailed information, please read the nonfiction introduction to *People of the Longhouse*.

Let's take a few moments to discuss the

Iroquoian perspective on captives. By the 1400s, as it was in historic times, warfare and raiding for captives was probably the most important method of gaining prestige in Northern Iroquoian societies. When a person died, the spiritual power of the clan was diminished, especially if that person had been a community leader. The places of missing family members literally remained vacant until they could be "replaced," and their spiritual power—which was embodied in their name—transferred to another person.

Historical records tell us that during the 1600s, the Iroquois dispatched war parties whose sole intent was to bring home captives to replace family members and restore the spiritual strength of the clans. These were called "mourning wars." Clan matrons usually organized the war parties and ordered their warriors to bring them captives suitable for adoption to assuage their grief and restock the village. When the captives arrived in the village, they were stripped, bound hand and foot, and forced to run a gauntlet where they were struck with clubs, burned with firebrands, cut with knives—but not killed.

After the torture, the tribal council assigned the captives to families that had lost loved ones to the enemy. Sometimes prisoner exchanges occurred, and the captives were returned to their own peoples, but usually one of two things happened:

They were either adopted into their new family, or the adoptive family could condemn the captive to death by torture. If he was adopted, he *might* be given the name and title of the dead person he replaced. Such adoptees underwent the Requickening Ceremony. In this ritual, the dead person's soul was "raised up" and transferred to the captive, along with his or her name.

This may seem odd to modern readers, but keep the religious context in mind. The Iroquois believed that each person had two souls. While specific traditions vary slightly, in general, the afterlife soul of those who died violently could not find the Path of Souls in the sky that led to the Land of the Dead. They were excluded from joining their ancestors in the afterlife and doomed to spend eternity wandering the earth. The souls of men and women killed in battles that were not "raised up" were believed, according to some Seneca traditions, to move into trees. It was these trees with indwelling warrior spirits that the People cut to serve as palisade logs, thereby surrounding the village with Standing Warriors.

Iroquoian oral history speaks of this as a particularly brutal time, a time when the Iroquois almost destroyed themselves, and clearly the archaeological record supports their stories.

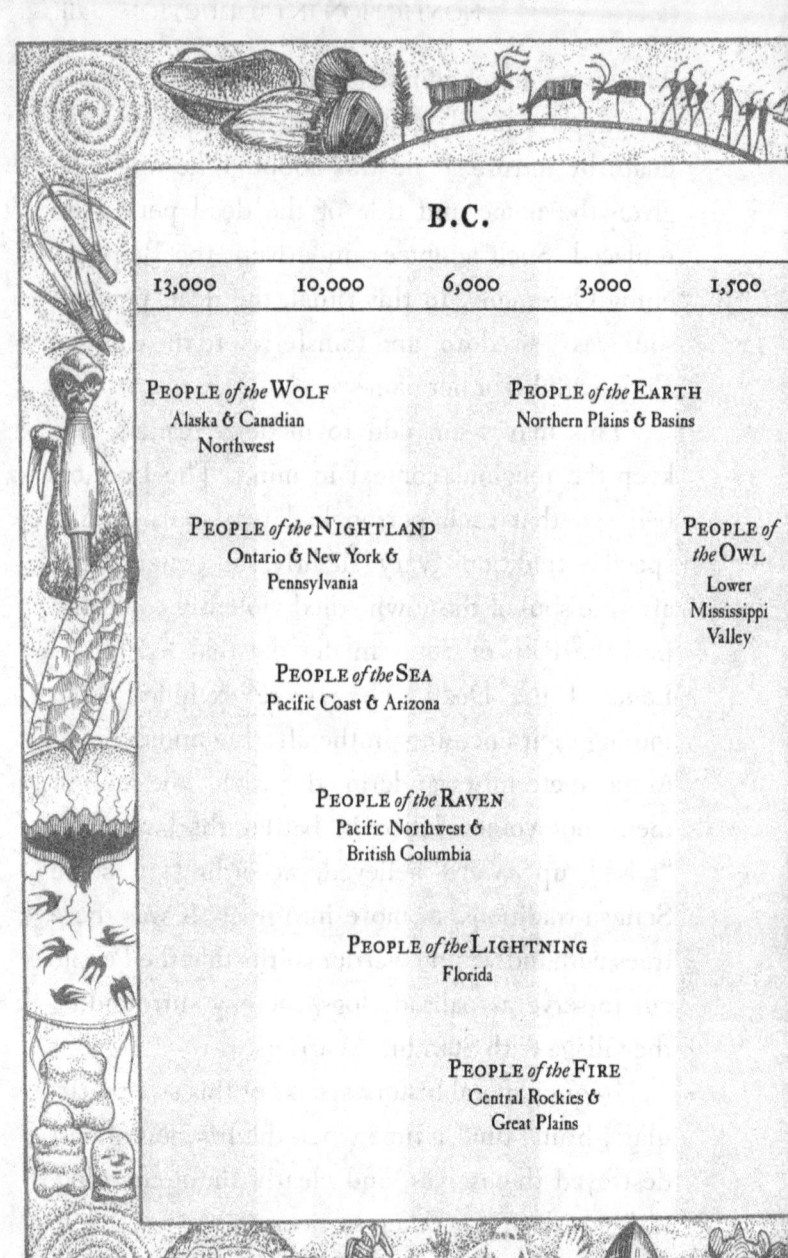

B.C.

13,000	10,000	6,000	3,000	1,500

PEOPLE *of the* **WOLF**
Alaska & Canadian
Northwest

PEOPLE *of the* **EARTH**
Northern Plains & Basins

PEOPLE *of the* **NIGHTLAND**
Ontario & New York &
Pennsylvania

PEOPLE *of*
the **OWL**
Lower
Mississippi
Valley

PEOPLE *of the* **SEA**
Pacific Coast & Arizona

PEOPLE *of the* **RAVEN**
Pacific Northwest &
British Columbia

PEOPLE *of the* **LIGHTNING**
Florida

PEOPLE *of the* **FIRE**
Central Rockies &
Great Plains

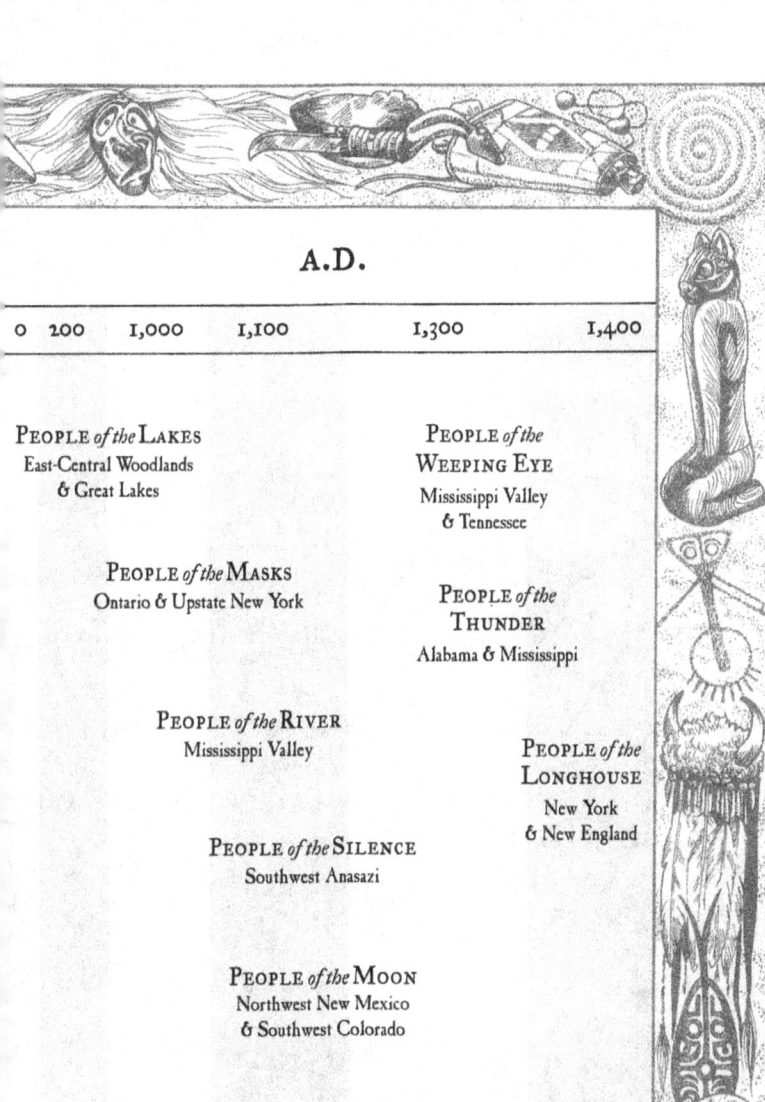

A.D.

| 0 | 200 | 1,000 | 1,100 | 1,300 | 1,400 |

PEOPLE *of the* LAKES
East-Central Woodlands
& Great Lakes

PEOPLE *of the*
WEEPING EYE
Mississippi Valley
& Tennessee

PEOPLE *of the* MASKS
Ontario & Upstate New York

PEOPLE *of the*
THUNDER
Alabama & Mississippi

PEOPLE *of the* RIVER
Mississippi Valley

PEOPLE *of the*
LONGHOUSE
New York
& New England

PEOPLE *of the* SILENCE
Southwest Anasazi

PEOPLE *of the* MOON
Northwest New Mexico
& Southwest Colorado

PEOPLE *of the* MIST
Chesapeake Bay

Skanodario Lake

Canassatego Village

IROQUOIA
The Lands of the
People of the
Longhouse

otarho Village
Yellowtail Village
Bur Oak Village   Forks River
White Dog Village   Singleleaf
                         Wild River   Village
                         Village

                                        Rapid River

The Lands of the
People of the
Dawnland

Forks River

Royal River

Quill River

Singleleaf
Village

Wild River
Village

Hawk Moth
Village

Bog
Willow
Village

Pine
Hill
Village

IROQUOIA

Rapid River

Quill River

THE DUSK COUNTRY

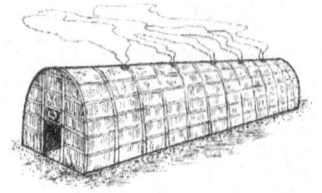

1

War Chief Cord sat behind Sindak in the rear of the lead canoe, paddling it around a rough bend in the river. Rocks thrust up here and there but were barely visible in the choppy current. They had to be careful. Close to shore, the leafless boughs of scarlet oaks overhung the water, casting black shadows over the fallen acorns that littered the bank.

From behind, Cord heard the War Chief of the Standing Stone People, Koracoo, call, "Deputy Gonda? Put ashore."

Gonda swung around and shouted, "What? Why? We're making good time!"

Cord, obeying her order, said, "Sindak, let's put ashore over there near the chokecherries. That looks like the best place."

While he and Sindak steered the canoe toward

the brush, Gonda glowered at them. Cord and Sindak leaped out of the boat as soon as they could and helped shove it up onto the sand. Almost instantly, Koracoo's canoe slid up beside them.

She jumped ashore and said, "We're stopping for a few hundred heartbeats. That's all. Eat something, drink, and do whatever else you must; then we're leaving."

Gonda said, "We shouldn't be stopping at all. Anything people need to do, they can—"

"That was not a request."

Gonda propped his hands on his hips to watch her as she walked away from him and went to stand beside Sindak. Cord glanced at Gonda. Koracoo and Gonda been arguing more and more, snapping at each other like warring turtles. Worse, the constant challenges to Koracoo's authority were undermining her credibility with her men. Cord had begun to notice that both Sindak and Towa were questioning her orders more often. If she didn't put a stop to this soon, she'd have a real problem on her hands.

Wakdanek, the children, and Towa disappeared into the trees to Cord's right.

Gonda strode over to Koracoo and Sindak. Each had pulled small bags of food from their belt pouches and were chewing in silence. "Koracoo, listen to me, you..."

Cord walked away.

The amber gleam of late afternoon coated the slender trunks of chokecherries that grew along the shore and glimmered from the river with blinding intensity.

He took the opportunity to walk upstream, where he could keep watch for canoes coming around the bend. They were well into territory belonging to the People Who Separated. The Quill River was broad and lazy, like an old woman who loved nothing better than to doze in the tree shadows. But occasional shallows ran swift and dangerous. By the time any pursuers saw their party, the enemy would have a hard time getting to shore. Still, he kept watch.

As he waded out to fill his water bag, he looked back at the group near the canoes. Wakdanek had joined the circle. One by one, the children filtered from the undergrowth and stood talking.

Cord lifted his water bag and took a long drink of the cool earthy water. He'd swallowed a stale cornmeal biscuit a short time ago. Hunger was at bay for the moment, but he had a powerful thirst. He emptied half the bag and filled it again. As he straightened, he heard Koracoo's distinctively soft steps. It was a faint almost-not-there sound, little more than grains of sand shifting.

"May I speak with you?" she said.

"Of course." He tied his water bag to his belt and turned.

Koracoo took a deep breath and let it out slowly while she gazed across the wide glistening river, as though considering her words, but she was also avoiding his eyes—and he knew why. He felt the attraction, too. But it was not the time for either of them. Their peoples were at war.

"I have a problem," she said.

"I know."

She turned to face him, and their gazes locked. They'd been paddling hard, and sweat had matted her short black hair to her cheeks, framing her large eyes and small nose. She had her legendary war club CorpseEye propped on her shoulder. Even from two paces away, he could sense a presence in the club, old and powerful. The carvings along the shaft added to the effect. The antlered wolves seemed to be chasing the winged tortoises, who were being chased by prancing buffalo. The red quartzite cobble tied to the top of the club reflected the light.

Her eyes tightened. "I didn't realize it was so obvious."

"Why don't you let me explain what I see, rather than having you tell me?"

"Go on."

Cord exhaled hard before he said, "It's clear that recently something has changed between the two of you. You want distance, but he still loves you. What appears to be anger on his part is actually, I believe, grief. He's finally realized that he's lost you, and it's tearing him apart. So...returning anger for anger will not solve the problem. But you must solve it. Quickly."

Their gazes held. Her eyes were as black and translucent as obsidian. It was strange for him to stand eye-to-eye with a woman. Very few were as tall as he was. And she had meltingly dark eyes.

"What is your recommendation?" she asked.

He frowned out at the water. "He's been your deputy for a long time?"

"Yes."

"Pick a new deputy. You need someone you can trust to give good orders in the worst of moments. Sindak, perhaps?"

Her eyes narrowed slightly. "Not you?"

"No. I'm an outsider from the Flint People. They won't listen to me."

She studied him for a long time, as though trying to read his souls.

A short distance from the shore, a flock of ducks floated, riding the swells as they chattered to each other. He watched them while he waited for her to think it over.

At last, she replied, "Gonda has been my right hand for thirteen summers. He knows my thoughts almost before I do."

"That's why this is so hard for him. He thinks you need him." Cord stared at her. Neither of them blinked. "It will be a kindness, Koracoo. He doesn't know how to step aside. Though I suspect he realizes he needs to."

The ducks suddenly took wing, squawking as they flapped away into the afternoon sky. Koracoo frowned at them for a time before she said, "He may, but this decision will still enrage him."

"Maybe. But eventually he'll understand why you did it."

Koracoo pulled CorpseEye off her shoulder and lovingly smoothed her fingers over the club as she thought. "I want you to serve as my deputy."

Cord shifted awkwardly. "I don't think that's a wise choice. Your men do not know me."

"Which means you will have to make an effort to get to know them."

"I can do that, but think hard before you—"

She walked away. As she neared the group, she called, "We're switching positions. Wakdanek, I want you with Towa in the rear of Gonda's canoe. Children, split up however you please, two in each canoe."

As the three men moved for their boat, Koracoo said, "Gonda, I need to speak with you."

She marched past him and led the way into a grove of larches. He followed her. Cord could just see them through the sunlit weave of yellow needles. Gonda had his head down, as though listening intently.

In the meantime, Odion and Baji climbed into Koracoo's canoe. The other two children got into Gonda's. Wakdanek and Towa stood at the bow, waiting.

Sindak was squinting at Koracoo and Gonda. From this angle, his hooked nose looked especially long.

Cord walked up beside him. "Sindak, go ahead and get in. As soon as Koracoo arrives, I'll shove us off. I'm already soaked to the knees."

"So am I." Sindak tucked his war club into his belt and folded his arms beneath his cape. Without looking at Cord, he said, "That sounded like an order. Did you and Koracoo have an interesting conversation?"

"We—"

A sharp *"What?"* erupted from the forest.

"That's my decision," Koracoo said. "You and I have been snarling at each other like rabid dogs."

"Why now?"

She said something no one could hear.

Branches cracked as Gonda thrashed his way through brush and shouted at Wakdanek and Towa, "Get in."

They leaped to obey, taking up positions in the rear. The boat rocked violently as Gonda shoved it off the sand and jumped into the bow. In less than five heartbeats, the man had maneuvered out into the current and was heading downriver.

Gonda hadn't even looked at Cord. But he would. By the end of the day, he'd be strutting around Cord like a stiff-legged dog. It was the way of men.

Koracoo walked out of the trees carrying CorpseEye in both hands, as though ready to bash anything that annoyed her.

Sindak's brows lifted. As Koracoo came across the sand, he said, "Gonda seemed a little upset."

She replied, "War Chief Cord is my new deputy. We're leaving." She stalked past him, climbed to the rear, and grabbed an oar.

Odion and Baji watched her with wide eyes. They knew better than to say anything. Odion clutched his wolf puppy tighter, and Gitchi wriggled unhappily.

Sindak turned to Cord. "Do you want to ride in the rear with her...or am I the condemned man?"

Cord smiled. "You're the condemned man."

Sindak heaved a sigh and got in.

Just as Cord started to shove the bow away from the shore, he heard something.

A soft suffocating cry.

Koracoo heard it, too. She straightened and shipped her paddle. "What was that?"

Odion got on his knees, listened for a few instants, and pointed to the larches to the south. "There, Mother." He swung around to make sure she'd heard him.

Koracoo nodded. "Cord, go east and come up behind the larches. I'll approach from the shore. Sindak, stay and guard the children."

"But Mother," Odion said. "It sounds like a child. Can I—?"

"No."

The boy sank back to the packs with a disappointed expression.

Cord unslung his bow, pulled an arrow from his quiver, and slipped silently to the edge of the trees before he nocked it. The larches were in the process of shedding their needles, but enough remained to create a fuzzy yellow halo that extended back indefinitely into the forest. As he entered the grove, the cry came again.

Gently, so that he made no sound, Cord eased aside the branch blocking his path and stepped by. He carefully returned the branch to its former position. It made only the slightest shishing as a handful of needles pattered the duff.

He studied the dense undergrowth of dogwoods to his left. The weeping penetrated the thicket, but just barely, as though the person had his face buried in a heavy blanket to muffle his cries.

Birds hopped through the branches above him, chirping, which helped to cover the crackling of the old larch needles as Cord edged toward the thicket.

When he reached the outermost edge of the

dogwoods, he saw movement and stood perfectly still, studying the shape until he made out what seemed to be four arms. Then eyes opened and stared at him.

"I'm not going to hurt you," he said in the Dawnland tongue. By now the child would have assessed his hairstyle and fitted wolfhide coat as those of a Flint warrior. He might even suspect that Cord had been involved in the attack on Bog Willow Village. Assuming the boy knew about it. They were far south of traditional Dawnland country. The news may not have reached here yet.

The boy lifted his head. He wore a ratty cape made from woven strips of weasel hide, and had a narrow face with a thin bladelike nose. Tears glued stringy black hair to his cheeks. Amid the dogwood limbs, he appeared to be perhaps eight or nine summers old. The boy's breathing sounded labored.

Cord struggled to decipher what he was seeing. When the boy shifted to sit up, his two arms became visible, but something wasn't right about the shapes. The body parts didn't seem to connect.

Cord released the tension on his bowstring and called, "Are you hungry? I have food I'll share with you."

Dark eyes blinked.

Nearby, Koracoo moved stealthily across the larch duff. If he hadn't known she was coming, he might have assumed the sound was nothing more than birds scratching through the fallen needles. She stopped. Perhaps because she'd seen the boy.

Cord slung his bow and crouched down where he could see beneath the dogwood branches. The boy was scared witless, trembling. Tears ran down his cheeks.

Cord extended a hand. "You're safe with us. Why don't you come out where we can talk?"

A shaking little-boy voice said, "I-I'm lost."

"It's all right. We'll help you. What's your name?"

The boy licked his lips nervously. "Toksus."

Koracoo slipped through the undergrowth and came to kneel beside Cord. "Toksus," she called, "I give you my oath that you are safe. I am War Chief Koracoo of Yellowtail Village. I—"

"Yellowtail?" Toksus scrambled from beneath the dogwoods. Old leaves covered his hair. He stood with his fists clenched. "Wrass' village?"

In an unnaturally calm voice, Koracoo said, "Do you know Wrass?"

"He's my friend." Toksus suspiciously glanced back and forth between them. "We—we were in the same canoe."

Cord could see the vein in Koracoo's throat pounding, but she looked utterly calm when she asked, "Did you escape from Gannajero, Toksus?"

The boy's chest spasmed with tears, and his face twisted. "She let me go."

Despite the fact that Koracoo must have had a thousand questions, she said only, "Then we need to get you home. What's your village?"

"It was a-attacked. I don't know if anyone's alive."

"Bog Willow Village?"

The boy nodded.

Koracoo said, "We were just there. Many survived. In fact, we're traveling with someone you may know. He was your village Healer, Wakdanek."

Toksus took a shocked step toward them. "He's my cousin. Where is he? I want to see him."

"He just shoved off in his canoe, but I'll send people to bring him back."

Koracoo slowly moved toward him. Toksus watched her like a small, frightened animal. When she was close enough, Koracoo reached out and stroked his hair. "You're going to be all right, Toksus. We'll get you home."

While Koracoo spoke with the boy, Cord tried to figure out the shapes beneath the dogwoods. Finally, he asked, "Toksus, who's the other boy?"

Toksus turned around to stare at the body half covered with leaves. "Sassacus. He—he was Partridge Clan."

Koracoo's face slackened as she connected the

apparently disparate shapes. "Dear gods, it's a body."

Toksus sobbed again and wiped his eyes on his sleeve. "I don't know how he got here. I ran all night. I was so tired, I had to nap. When I woke up a little while ago, he was lying beside me. It scared me."

"Is that why you covered him with leaves?"

He croaked, "I was afraid he'd followed me."

Cord was confused by the statement, but Koracoo stroked the boy's hair again and softly asked, "Did you see him witched?"

Toksus' mouth opened and his chest heaved, but no sound came out.

Koracoo pulled him into her arms. The boy wept, "She killed him! Stabbed him in the back. Then she—she..."

When he couldn't go on, Koracoo hugged him tighter and turned to Cord. "Ask Odion and Baji to come over here, then take the canoe. Catch Gonda. With the current, it'll probably be easier for Sindak to lead Wakdanek back along the shore. I want you and Gonda to remain and guard the canoes."

"Understood."

Cord sprinted away, ducked the low branches of the larches, and thrashed through the brush. When he appeared on the shore, he noticed that Sindak had gotten out of the canoe and nocked his bow. He stood guard a few paces from the children.

"Good man, Sindak."

Sindak's brows plunged down over his hooked nose. "We heard a boy's voice. Who is he?"

"He's a Dawnland child. One of the survivors of the Bog Willow battle. I'll tell you more later. Right now, we have catch Gonda."

As Cord grabbed an oar, he said, "Odion, Baji, the war chief wants you to join her."

Odion and Baji scrambled out of the canoe and ran away with Odion calling, *"Mother?* Where are you?"

Cord shoved the bow away from the sand, and said, "Come on, Sindak. We have our work cut out catching Gonda."

2

Wrass sat on the sandy, leaf-strewn bank with his hands tied behind his back. His balance was off. He kept falling over, then righting himself, trying to stay upright. The agony in his head was unbearable, but his ankle hurt worse.

Gannajero's four warriors had formed a tight circle three paces away. Though their voices were low, their grim expressions told him more than words. At least one of them was on the verge of bolting into the wilderness at the first opportunity.

"The boy is useless," Dakion said. He gestured with his war club, and his buckskin cape flared and buffeted in the wind. His broad muscular shoulders strained against his cape. "We should crack his skull and leave him for the wolves. We can find new children anywhere."

Ojib responded, "Even in his condition, he'll bring a few trinkets."

"But he's more trouble than he's worth! He can hardly walk now. I think he broke his ankle in the fall."

Waswan used the back of his hand to wipe his knobby nose and straightened his sapling-thin body to glare at Dakion. "The boy is *her* property. She decides what to do with him."

Wrass looked down at his foot. His ankle was badly swollen and had turned a mottled reddish purple, but he didn't think it was broken. Just badly sprained. The thick bed of leaves had cushioned his fall, and probably saved his life. He just couldn't put his weight on the ankle. One thing was certain—his hope of escape was gone. He wouldn't be able to run for days, maybe longer. The despair that filled him was like an animal eating him from the inside out.

He let his aching head fall forward. It didn't matter. Zateri and the Dawnland girls had gotten away. That made seven children Gannajero had lost in just a few days. The old witch was furious.

Dakion turned to Kotin. "Kotin, we should be far south by now. What if those girls walk into a nearby village and tell them they were held captive by Gannajero the Crow? The chief will organize a war party of hundreds to come looking for us. We need to put distance between us and—"

"Didn't you hear what Waswan said? It's *her* decision!" Kotin snarled, and jerked his head toward Gannajero.

Back in the trees, she stood bent over, working on something on the ground. She kept making small grunts, as though it was hard labor. Occasionally she lifted her knife high enough that the white chert blade glinted in the sunlight.

"What's she doing?" Dakion said. "She won't let any of us get close. Is she—?"

Ojib interrupted. "I'm more worried about that messenger who came to see her. Why won't she tell us what he said?"

"Maybe because it's none of our concern," Kotin replied. "The message was for her."

"But how did the man know where she was? He must have followed us from the big warriors' camp. If so much as a single person there recognized her"—Dakion waved an arm extravagantly—" there could be fifty canoes searching for us this instant!"

Kotin shook his head, but it was so faint Wrass doubted the other warriors noticed. Revealing broken yellow teeth, he said, "If there were, I promise you, she'd know it."

"You give her too much credit. She's just an old woman. She has no powers or the children would never have been able to escape. We'd already be far south and safely away…"

His voice faded when Gannajero abruptly stood up. Everyone saw her lift the dead boy's severed eyeballs. They had shriveled and turned opaque. She held one eyeball in each hand and was slowly turning around in a circle, murmuring. When she stopped turning, she let out a sharp gleeful laugh and stared off to the north.

"I don't like this," Dakion hissed. "She just does these bizarre things to scare us."

Gannajero put the eyes back in her belt pouch. Then she bent down, draped something over her left arm, and started toward them. Whatever she carried was long enough to drag on the ground. It slurred wetly over the leaves.

Dakion shook a fist at Kotin. "We have to do something now, before she—"

"Are you the hero, Dakion?" Gannajero asked in a low menacing voice as she emerged from the trees.

"What?"

She walked into the clearing, and Wrass frowned at the thing draped over her arm. Slowly, like poison working through his veins, he realized it was a human skin. Thin and coated with blood, the arms and legs swung as she walked. Revulsion wrenched a small cry of horror from his throat. He scrambled backward, trying to get as far from her as he could.

"I'll let you be the hero, Dakion," she said with

mock kindness. She'd started to tiptoe forward, like a hunting cat. "You should have asked."

In less than a heartbeat, Dakion had his war club in his fist. "You're crazy, old woman!"

"Yes, I am doomed to walk this earth alone forever, so I have nothing to lose." Her toothless mouth widened. "What about you?"

Dakion swallowed hard. "The boy is worthless. Just tell me why we can't kill him?"

Gannajero's smile froze on her wrinkled face. Without taking her gaze from him, she said, "She'll come for him."

"Who will? What are you talking about? There could be one hundred canoes on the river behind us, chasing us down, and all you can do is blather nonsense? Just let me kill the boy, so he doesn't slow us—"

"I've already told you I'll let you be the hero. Why are you still so worried about the boy?" She cocked her head in that strange birdlike manner, eyeing him first through one eye, then the other.

Dakion appeared totally confused. He took another grip on his club as though the shaft had grown slick with sweat.

The other warriors backed away. Kotin, in particular, looked terrified.

"The boy"—Gannajero gave Dakion a cruel toothless grin—" is mine. Understand?"

Dakion looked as though he might burst at the

seams. He waved his war club threateningly. "What are you going to do with him? Is he a hostage? Why won't you tell us what the messenger said? What are you hiding?"

An old hatred, something grown fine and sharp over the long summers, flickered in her black eyes. "The messenger said that my brother promises me wealth and power beyond my imaginings. Would you like to share in that?"

"Your brother?" Dakion said. "Who is he? How rich is he?"

The old woman scanned the faces of her warriors. "Anyone who wishes can walk away now with no punishment." She adjusted the limp skin over her arm. "Go on. Get out of my sight. But anyone who chooses to stay will be richly rewarded."

The men glanced at each other. She'd already bestowed enough wealth upon them to make them very rich men. Wrass studied the gleam that came to each man's eyes. How could they still want more?

"So," Gannajero said. "No one wishes to leave."

They shifted; someone mumbled; all of them glanced at the skin over her arm.

"Then get out of my way," she growled.

She walked through the middle of their circle. Men stumbled backward to clear a path for her. As she knelt and began rinsing the skin in the river, graying black hair flopped around her wrinkled face.

Kotin gave the other three men an evil look. "I've been with her a long time, and she's never failed to keep her promises. In a few short moons, you could all have enough wealth to ransom a village. Keep that in mind the next time you threaten to betray her."

Wrass—beside the maple tree—saw Gannajero smile.

Dakion kicked at an old branch. "She'd better keep her promise. I expect to live long enough to enjoy my earnings."

Gannajero stood up and stretched the clean, dripping skin out from arm to arm. Without turning she called, "Who would like to help me make a frame? As soon as he's dry, I'll enchant him. Then we'll leave."

Kotin and Ojib trotted to her side. Dakion shook his head. Dust swirled and sparkled faintly in the still air around him.

With practiced ease, Gannajero collected and tied together four long sticks of driftwood, creating a rectangular frame. Ojib and Kotin then helped Gannajero stretch the feet, hands, and neck into place to keep the skin taut while it dried. The vaguely human-shaped skin continued to drip onto the old leaves.

The shape fascinated Wrass. He couldn't take his eyes from it. The old woman had skinned Akio as a man would a deer, her knife slitting up from the ankle to the groin, then peeling back the skin. The legs and arms appeared to be twice as wide as they had been when alive and sheathing muscles. Only the head was missing.

Something clinked. Wrass' gaze shot back to Gannajero as she pulled a beautiful copper bell from her belt pouch. Pounded into a thin sheet then twisted into a cone, such copper bells were traditionally used to adorn the moccasins of cere-monial dancers. A shell bead was hung in the center of the cone and made it tinkle pleasantly.

Dakion shouted, "Where did you get that? That's mine!"

He tramped over to where his pack rested in the canoe and began digging through it, searching, as though to make certain.

While he occupied himself, Gannajero carried the bell to the skinned neck and tied it on. Even the slightest breath of wind encouraged it to make music.

Dakion roared, "You took it!"

Gannajero touched the bell with gnarled fingers. It had been polished to a beautiful sheen. She took a few moments to stare at it before she glanced at the other warriors and whispered, "It's like giving a fresh fox skin to a dog just before the hunt. By the time you release the dog, he's so desperate for the taste of fox blood that he's lunging at his tether and frothing at the mouth."

Fear prickled Wrass' skin. What was she talking about?

Dakion climbed out of the canoe and stalked back with his club swinging. "Why did you tie it to the skin? Give it to me." He extended his hand.

Gannajero laughed softly. "I'm training a new dog."

"A dog? Are you calling me a dog?"

She smiled, but it didn't reach her eyes. "This *hanehwa* has one duty. No matter where you go, he'll track you down and tell me where you are."

As the implications sank in, Dakion's extended hand slowly clenched to a fist. Where only moments before he'd scoffed at her powers, now he licked his lips and his eyes darted to the others. "She's insane. I don't believe any of this."

"Yes, I can see that." Gannajero straightened, and the shells and twists of copper on her cape flashed. "Kotin, untie Hawk-Face. He can't run. Then bring the skin and come find me. I want to talk to you. Alone."

"Yes, Gannajero."

Kotin quickly walked over and slit the ropes tying Wrass' hands. "Don't try anything stupid," he growled.

Wrass struggled to give him a defiant glare. "I can't even walk. How could I?"

Kotin turned away and went to retrieve the frame with the stretched skin. As he walked back into the trees where Gannajero stared up at the sky, the old woman said, "Hang it up there where it can dry in the sunlight."

The other warriors gathered around Dakion, whispering ominously.

Wrass hadn't had any water since dawn. He gazed longingly at the river, but when he tried to put weight on his ankle it felt like fiery splinters were being driven into his flesh.

Wrass rolled to his hands and knees and started crawling for the water. The entire time, Dakion watched him hatefully.

Tears blurred his eyes. While he'd badly injured his ankle in the fall, every part of him hurt. His ribs felt as though the muscles had been pulled loose from the bones.

When he finally reached the water, he greedily scooped it into his mouth with his hand. Rivulets spilled down his chin, but he kept drinking until he could hold no more. There was no telling when he'd get to drink again.

Wrass rolled to his back and, for a few blessed moments, lay on the riverbank staring up at the gathering Cloud People. The blue-black giants were pushing eastward.

"Load up," Gannajero's gravelly voice rasped. "We're heading south."

She and Kotin tramped past Wrass without even glancing at him. It was as though he no longer existed. Gannajero climbed into the bow of the lead canoe and irritably watched her men stow their gear. "Come on. We're in a hurry!"

Ojib clambered for the rear of Gannajero's canoe and picked up a paddle, while Waswan settled into the rear of the other canoe. Dakion and Kotin remained on shore to push off.

As Kotin shoved the lead canoe into the current and leaped into the bow, Dakion glanced at Wrass and shouted, "Wait! What about the boy? Is he riding in my canoe?"

"We're leaving him," Gannajero answered, just before the river grabbed hold of her canoe and carried it downstream.

"I don't believe it!" Dakion gestured wildly to Waswan. "She'd planned all along to leave him? Why didn't she just tell me?"

Waswan chuckled, and his small inhuman eyes glinted. "She probably thought it was none of your business."

Dakion shook his head, shoved the canoe into the river, and jumped in. As they paddled out into the current, Wrass heard Dakion say, "With all the starving wolves in this country, that boy will be dead by nightfall."

Wrass shoved up on one elbow to watch them disappear around the bend.

Stunned, an odd floating sensation came over him. They'd left him. He was free. Before he realized it, tears warmed his face. He could...he could go home! It might take him a while, but if he splinted and wrapped his ankle, he'd make it. There were many good walking sticks in sight. A fallen maple branch about his height lay less than ten paces away.

A few instants later, when he tried to stand up, reality returned with a vengeance. His ankle went out from under him, and he landed hard on the sand. Grabbing his screaming ankle, he rocked back and forth. The swelling was worse. Only a hand of time ago, he'd been able to fit both his hands around the joint.

Fear seeped through his relief and joy.

Dakion had been right. Many large predators ran along this shore. It was a primary hunting trail for wolves, bears, and cougars.

Wrass looked back into the trees. He couldn't see it, but he knew it wouldn't take the wolves long to catch the scent of Akio's freshly skinned corpse.

He had to get as far away from here as he could.

3

"Gonda! Wait!"

Gonda spun around at the call and pulled his oar out of the water. In the rear, Towa and Wakdanek turned to watch the approaching canoe. Sindak and Cord were stroking hard, trying to catch them. Their canoe shot forward, piercing the green water like an arrow.

Gonda realized that Koracoo and the children were missing, and he shouted, "Put ashore. Hurry. Something's wrong!"

Wakdanek and Towa backed water, turning the canoe; then they all fought the current to head to a small spit of sand on the eastern shore. Thick willows filled in the spaces between the towering trees. The spit was the only place to land. Gonda leaped out as they glided in and helped drag the boat up onto the bank. As the cold shadows of the trees enveloped him, a thousand possible explanations for Koracoo and the children's absence skittered across his souls—none of them good.

As the canoe sliced through the water toward them, Tutelo got on her knees, and called, "Father? Where's Mother? Where's Odion and Baji?"

"I'm sure they're fine," he answered. "You and Hehaka can get out. Just stay close."

"Yes, Father."

Tutelo's long braid switched across her back as she climbed over packs and oars to get out of the canoe. Hehaka followed more slowly, but both children ended up standing beside Gonda, staring up at him worriedly.

Towa and Wakdanek slogged ashore and waited beside the canoe.

Gonda yelled, "Where are Koracoo and the children? What happened?"

Cord shipped his paddle and shouted back, "We found a Dawnland boy. They stayed with him while we came after you."

"A boy?" Wakdanek called. "Who is he?"

Sindak's canoe grounded with a loud grating sound. As Cord jumped into the water and waded ashore, he answered, "The child was hiding thirty paces from our camp."

The two feathers on Wakdanek's moosehide hat wafted in the wind as he closed on Cord. "What's his name?"

"He said he was your cousin. His name is Toksus."

Wakdanek straightened. "Blessed gods! Is he all right?" He ran forward.

"He appears to be, but Koracoo wants you there immediately. Sindak will guide the rest of you back. Gonda and I will remain here to guard the canoes."

Gonda vented a low ugly laugh. "I'm not staying here. You can guard the canoes by yourself. I want to talk to the boy. How did he get this far south? What—?"

Cord turned to Sindak. "Hurry. We know we're on the right path now. The sooner we're on the water again, the sooner we'll catch Gannajero."

Sindak dipped his head in a nod and called, "Everyone, follow me."

Towa, Wakdanek, and the children gathered around Sindak.

When Gonda started to join Sindak's group, Cord caught him by the arm and forcibly pulled him back. "These aren't my orders. They're hers."

Gonda's muscles bulged as he shook off Cord's restraining hand. Murderous rage was filling him up, threatening to burst loose in a frenzy of fists or clashing war clubs. It took every bit of strength he had to calm himself enough to say through gritted teeth, "She did this on purpose, you know."

Cord just stared at him. "What?"

"Left us here together."

"Why would that be?"

"Don't be a dimwit. You've seen how she splits up her warriors."

Cord appeared to think about that for a moment; then the knife scar that cut across his jaw tilted up in admiration. "Yes. I've marveled at it. Or rather, marveled at the fact that it seems to work. I would never separate friends and create teams of enemies. I'd be afraid they'd kill each other before they arrived at some sort of reconciliation."

"This time her strategy isn't going to work."

"Why not?"

"I'm not going to get over being demoted and having an enemy warrior installed in my place—even if I do come to respect him."

Cord's mouth set into a grim line. "I'm not sure I would either."

As his anger began to drain away, Gonda had to clench his jaw to steady his nerves. He said, "Tell me what happened with the child. How did you find him?"

Cord's wary attention remained on the river, the trees. "Just before we shoved off we heard him crying. He was hiding, entangled with a corpse, beneath a thicket of dogwoods."

"A corpse?"

"Yes, there were actually two Dawnland children—one was dead."

"What killed him?"

As though to ease his tension, Cord ran a hand over the black roach of hair that lined the top of his head. Several yellow larch needles fell out. "The living boy, Toksus, said that the dead boy had been witched, and then stabbed, by Gannajero."

"Gannajero? Toksus was with Gannajero?" Panic tingled Gonda's veins. He grabbed Cord's arm. "H-How long ago?"

"Yesterday."

"So she's just ahead of us on the river?" He swung around to look downstream, as though expecting to see her canoes. Only swaying maples met his gaze. A few old leaves blew from the branches and fluttered into the rushing water.

"Apparently."

"The other children with her, what did Toksus—?"

"He said he'd talked to Wrass. That's all. But we shouldn't make too much of that. Koracoo ordered me to find you, and I left immediately."

Gonda felt light-headed. He took a few steps away from Cord and struggled to control his hope. What would Koracoo be thinking? She'd be vacillating, wondering what to do with the Dawnland child. They couldn't just leave him wandering alone in the forest. It was inhuman. The boy had been through unimaginable terrors. He needed to go home to his family...whatever was left of it. But they didn't have the luxury of turning around and taking the boy home. They had to...

"It will be a problem." Cord still had his attention focused on the trees.

"What will?" Gonda turned around.

"Another child."

It didn't surprise him that the Flint war chief was worried about the same thing he was. The danger increased tenfold with every additional child: more noise, more distractions, more chances that they'd all be killed.

Gonda gave the man an annoyed look. "So... what am I supposed to call you now? War Chief Cord or Deputy Cord?"

Cord calmly responded, "Our duty is to rescue the children, Gonda. She asked me. Not the reverse. And since she did, I plan to carry out my responsibilities to the best of my ability. You can call me whatever you like."

Gonda had the irrational desire to shout at him, which was sheer foolishness. Instead, he shook his fists at nothing and said, "I know this isn't your fault. I just...I thought Koracoo and I had resolved our differences. Obviously, I was wrong."

After a long pause, Cord asked, "What happened between you, Gonda?"

Taken aback by the boldness of the question, Gonda snapped, "What makes you think I'd tell you?"

Cord lifted a shoulder. "I'll find out anyway, but it will come from Sindak or Towa. Maybe small details from the children. Is that who you want to tell me?"

Gonda felt slightly ill. It was actually chilling to imagine Sindak relating the story of the fall of Yellowtail Village. He rubbed his forehead. "I disobeyed one of Koracoo's orders."

Cord shifted slightly. "Why?"

"*Why?* Because she was wrong. She wasn't there. I was. I had to make a decision."

"And what happened as a result?"

Gonda laughed softly, more in despair than amusement. "Do you know Yenda?"

Cord's mouth puckered. "The Mountain People's war chief? I've fought him many times. He's a worthless, arrogant fool. Why?"

Gonda searched the surrounding forest before he replied, "On the morning of the attack, a Trader came through bearing news that he'd heard Yenda was skulking around Yellowtail Village with a huge war party. The rumor could have been false. Koracoo, however, leaves nothing to chance. She took half our warriors out to investigate. She left me in charge of the village defense."

"Was your 'decision' the reason the village was destroyed?"

Images of the battle flooded through Gonda. He saw again the dead piling up in the plaza, heard the screams and cries of the wounded...felt the palisade catwalk shake as the onslaught of warriors hit it. He squeezed his eyes closed.

Finally, Cord asked, "How many warriors did Yenda have?"

"I'm not sure. My scouts reported somewhere around one thousand. But they were terrified; they could have exaggerated."

"How many did you have?"

"Three hundred."

When Gonda opened his eyes, he found Cord staring at him in sympathy. "So...in the last desperate moments something changed that made you disobey Koracoo's order. What was her order?"

Gonda crossed his arms over his aching heart and gazed out at the river, where an uprooted tree bobbed along in the current. As it rolled over, whole branches spun up and glittered in the sunlight. "Before she left, Koracoo ordered me to keep everyone inside the palisade. She feared that if I split my forces by sending even a handful of warriors outside, I'd never be able to hold the palisade."

"Was she right?"

"At the time, it seemed the only hope of saving a few of our people."

"So, you split your forces?"

"Yes, but I didn't make the decision hastily. I waited until the last possible moment. The palisade had been burned through in fifty places. Mountain warriors were crawling in and out like rats in a corn bin. Every longhouse was on fire."

Cord's gaze took on a faraway look, as though he was seeing it all play out on the fabric of his souls. "How many men did you send outside?"

"I led one hundred warriors out with our women and children, hoping we'd be able to protect them long enough that some could escape."

Cord didn't say anything.

Through a long exhalation, Gonda finished, "Everything fell apart. The village was overrun. Most of the warriors I'd led outside were killed, and many of the women and children were rounded up and marched away as slaves. Including my own children." The incapacitating ache he'd been suppressing swelled around his heart.

"Did some escape?"

"Yes. But not many."

Cord rubbed his chin with the back of his hand and nodded. "And when Koracoo returned, what did she do?"

"She found me in the forest, held me tightly while I wept...then she walked back into the village and started questioning people. She listened to the stories told by our remaining elders, talked to the people I'd left to guard the palisade, and questioned the few surviving warriors who'd gone outside with me. They all agreed I was to blame.

They said I should have never split my forces. After that, Koracoo marched straight to the smoldering husk of our longhouse, gathered what remained of my belongings, and set them outside the door. We'd been joined for twelve summers, and she divorced me without ever asking me a single question."

A thousand summers from now as he slumbered in an old oak tree, that wound would still be bleeding. To make matters worse, his heartache was suffocating him. He'd do anything to be able to hold her in his arms again.

A gust of wind rattled the branches, and a whirlwind of old leaves swept out across the river. Gonda watched them settle upon the surface. Like a fleet of tiny rafts, the current swiftly carried them downstream.

Cord said, "I know it means nothing now, but I doubt that splitting your forces is what caused the destruction of Yellowtail Village. If I'd been in your situation, outnumbered three to one, with the village collapsing around me, I would probably have taken the same desperate risk you did. By the time you made the decision, the battle was already lost. It was the only thing you could have done."

For a brief instant, Gonda's pain lessened. He had the feeling Cord meant it.

"Well, you would be wise not to mention that

to Koracoo. She'll demote you and name Sindak as her new deputy."

Cord smiled. "Actually, I suggested him for the position. I think he'd make a good one."

"Yes, well, you don't know him very well yet. He's young."

Cord dipped his head in deference to Gonda's experience. "If you say so."

In irritation, Gonda unslung his bow and pulled an arrow from his quiver. As he nocked it, he said, "I've had enough of making friends with you. I feel like killing something. Let's hunt."

Cord shook his head. "Koracoo ordered us to guard the canoes. However, I have no objections to allowing you to hunt, providing you stay within sight of the canoes. Agreed?"

Gonda jerked a nod. "Agreed...Deputy."

4

Koracoo stood guard two paces from where Odion, Baji, and Toksus sat talking. Now and then, one of them jerked around to look out into the larches, as though certain Gannajero and her warriors were sneaking up on them.

Koracoo understood the feeling. Toksus might well be bait for a trap. His story about how he'd gotten here was curious enough, but his insistence that he'd awakened beside the dead boy was truly bizarre.

She clutched CorpseEye and started walking in a small circle around the children, studying the ground for tracks. If Toksus wasn't making it up, someone must have placed Sassacus' body beside him. Who? Why? Had someone been trying to frighten Toksus? That seemed unlikely. Perhaps in some twisted way, Sassacus had been a gift. Company for a lost little boy? Or something more sinister. A warning not to tell anyone what had happened to him?

"Did you actually see Zateri?" Odion asked. He smoothed his shoulder-length black hair behind his ears. Sunlight falling through the branches striped his round face. "You're sure she was all right?"

Toksus pulled open the laces on a bag he carried and drew out a handful of huckleberries. As he chewed them, he said, "The last time I saw her, she was fine. Then the canoes shoved away from shore and went off down the river, leaving me alone."

"You were smart, Toksus," Odion praised. "You knew to walk straight north along the river. You weren't really lost. In a few more days, you'd have been home."

Toksus swallowed his huckleberries and plucked another handful from the bag. "I was so scared."

"Well, you're with us now. My parents will take you home."

Toksus chewed the berries in silence, as though he wasn't sure whether or not to believe it.

Baji was eyeing Toksus severely. She said, "How did you escape?"

"I didn't escape. Gannajero let me go."

"She's never let a child go in her life. They're worth too much. Why you?"

The next handful of huckleberries stopped halfway to Toksus's mouth. He lowered it back to his lap. "After she stabbed the dead boy, she dragged him over and put him on top of me. She..." His eyes went vacant, as though his afterlife soul had briefly been scared from his body.

In a dire voice, Odion said, "Why did she do that?"

Toksus waved the fist of huckleberries, but it was a weak gesture, as though his strength had vanished in an instant. "She was witching us."

"Both of you? Why?"

Toksus' fingers seemed to go numb. The berries dropped from his hand, and he began rubbing his palms on his leggings, as though to rid them of an unseen taint. When his eyes started rolling around in terror, Odion slid closer to him.

"Toksus, don't worry. You're safe. We're just trying to understand..."

Their voices faded as Koracoo's attention was captured by a set of tracks almost hidden beneath the dogwood boughs. She walked over and knelt near them, wary not to disturb the ground. As she used CorpseEye to lift a section of branches, her breath caught. The dense thicket had sheltered the earth from windblown needles and leaves. And the ground had been damp when he'd stepped here.

There were two tracks. Both clearly visible.

Her gaze lifted and swiftly examined the area. Was he still here? The tracks looked fresh. No rim of frost outlined the shapes, and there was no ice in the bottom of the tracks. They'd been made after the day had warmed with sunlight.

She edged closer and bent to examine them more carefully. The weather had turned cold and wet, but these were not moccasin prints. He was wearing sandals—the distinctive herringbone pattern woven only by the Hills People.

"She put his *soul* in me," Toksus wailed.

Koracoo lifted her head. Odion had gone pale.

Baji said, "Why did she want you to have the dead boy's soul?"

"I don't know. She said, 'Find him for me.' But I didn't know what she meant."

Baji cupped a hand to Odion's ear and whispered something. Odion nodded; then he swiveled around to face Toksus again. The boy looked at Odion as though afraid he was about to be left alone. He suddenly reached out and grabbed hold of Odion's sleeve.

"It wasn't my fault," Toksus explained. "I didn't do anything bad."

"She's a witch, Toksus," Odion said. "You're not to blame for what she does. Was she trying—?"

"She cut out his eyes, too."

Odion and Baji both looked at Koracoo, as though silently begging for an explanation.

She rose and retraced her tracks to where they sat in a circle. Toksus had started to cry. His chest heaved, and soft whimpers vibrated in his throat. The sight of him wrenched Koracoo's heart.

Baji said, "War Chief, have you ever heard of the ritual he described?"

"It's witch Power, Baji, evil. I know little about such things."

Baji's delicate brows lowered. She examined Koracoo as though she suspected she was lying, that she really did know but was withholding the information. Baji resented being treated like a child.

Koracoo relented and said, "She was probably trying to force Toksus to catch the dying boy's last breath. But Wakdanek is more familiar with such things. When he arrives, we'll—"

A shudder went through CorpseEye, and he warmed in her hands. As the heat increased, she shifted the club to her other hand. He was old and wise in the ways of the unseen forces that moved through the forest. *He sees something I don't.*

Her gaze swept upward from the bases of the trees to the highest limbs, then down to the brush, searching for any color or shape anomaly that would signal a hidden enemy warrior.

Very softly, so as not to startle her, Odion said,

"Mother, what's wrong?" He glanced at CorpseEye.

She touched her lips with her fingers, telling the children to be quiet. They reacted like grouse chicks at the sound of a wolf's stealthy paws, their muscles bunched, ready to scatter to the heavens.

When the breeze picked up, the larches swayed and creaked, and a shower of yellow needles cascaded from the sky. Koracoo kept her eyes on the most likely places a war party might burst from cover.

After twenty or thirty heartbeats, Odion lifted his chin and his nostrils flared.

Then Koracoo caught the scent. It smelled faintly like the foul miasma that hovers around week-old carcasses in the summertime. She turned into the wind to see if she could pinpoint where it was coming from...and heard steps.

With ghostly silence, she rose and spread her feet, then grasped CorpseEye in both hands.

"*Koracoo?*" Sindak called. "Where are you?"

She relaxed. "Over here, Sindak. In the larch grove."

A short while later, Sindak and Wakdanek emerged from the trees, followed by Tutelo and Hehaka. Towa brought up the rear.

Wakdanek called, "Toksus?"

The little boy leaped to his feet. "Cousin Wakdanek!"

Wakdanek knelt, and Toksus ran into his arms, weeping. "I thought you were dead. I thought everybody was dead!"

"No, Toksus." Wakdanek stroked his back gently. "Many of us survived. Your mother is alive. I saw her just a few hands of time ago. She'll be so happy to see you."

Toksus sobbed against Wakdanek's broad shoulder. "I didn't think I'd ever see my family again."

"Well, you will. Now, tell me how you got here, little cousin? You're a long way from home."

Toksus pulled away and wiped his nose on his sleeve. As the wind gusted, tree shadows painted his face. "Just after the battle, that ugly Flint Trader bought us, then sold us—"

"Bought who? How many Bog Willow children were with you?" The desperation in his voice was painful. "Was Conkesema—?"

"There were four of us. Me, Auma, Conkesema, and the dead boy."

At the sound of his daughter's name, tears entered the big raw-boned Healer's eyes. He made an effort to swallow them and said, "Is everyone else—?"

"They're still Gannajero's slaves." As though he couldn't keep his eyes away, Toksus turned to the half-buried body beneath the dogwoods.

"Who is he, Toksus?"

The boy whimpered, "Sassacus."

Wakdanek rose and went to crouch beside the body. He examined it for a long time before he grabbed one of the feet and pulled the boy out into the amber gleam. As he brushed dirt from the child's face, his heavy brows knitted into a single line. The boy's empty eye sockets were clotted with old blood.

Koracoo said, "Do you know him?"

Wakdanek jerked a nod. "What happened—?"

Toksus rushed to answer. "Gannajero stabbed him; then she dragged him over and put him on my chest, and she—"

"Did she put your mouths together, Cousin?"

Toksus jerked a nod and twined his fist in the shirt over his chest. "Ever since, I've felt something inside me, coiling around."

Wakdanek's expression slackened. He rose to his feet and went back to embrace Toksus. "It's all right. I brought ghost medicine with me. We'll banish his soul from your body, and you'll start getting stronger right away."

"Thank you. I'm so scared." Toksus propped his chin on Wakdanek's shoulder, and a peaceful expression came over his young face.

Koracoo said, "After she forced Toksus to catch his last breath, she cut out the dead boy's eyes. Do you know why?"

"It's witchery," Wakdanek replied. "Who can say why?"

He hugged Toksus again and released him; then he tilted his head to Koracoo, gesturing that they step away.

She followed him into a small clearing where the sound of the river was louder and she could smell the mossy fragrance of the water. "Now tell me the rest."

Wakdanek crossed his arms tightly over his chest. "I've heard of the ritual. A witch transfers someone's soul to another body, but keeps his eyes. No matter where the afterlife soul travels in its new body, the eyes can still see whatever the soul sees. In this case, the soul she placed in Toksus is seeing us."

A creeping sensation worked its way up her spine to the back of her neck. "You mean she could be using the dead boy's eyes to watch us right now?"

"It's possible. But it takes a very powerful witch to do such a thing, and I doubt..."

A scream rent the afternoon. They both lurched through the brush in time to see Toksus topple to the ground with his jaws snapping together like a rabid dog's. He began jerking violently, locked in a seizure.

Sindak and Towa were on him instantly,

holding his arms down so he couldn't hurt himself. Sindak cried, "Wakdanek!"

As the Healer ran, the children scrambled back, and Hehaka started yelling, "I didn't do anything! I swear it! He just fell down. I didn't even touch him!"

"What happened?" Wakdanek grabbed the boy's contorted face and stared into his rolling eyes. "Did he say anything?"

"No!" Odion shook his head. "He just asked Hehaka his name, and when Hehaka told him, Toksus got a strange look on his face..."

The seizure stopped. As Toksus's body began to go limp, his jaw gaped and his head lolled to the side.

"Toksus?" Wakdanek fell to the ground and put his ear over the boy's chest. "No. No!"

Sindak and Towa rose and backed away as Wakdanek grabbed Toksus beneath the arms, lifted him, and shook him hard, crying, "Toksus, breathe!"

Sindak followed Towa over to where Koracoo stood. Though Towa had left his waist-length hair loose, Sindak had tied his back with a leather cord. The style made his narrow face look even more aquiline.

Sindak murmured, "That looked very much like the effects of poison."

Only Koracoo's eyes moved as she met his hard gaze. "You think it's retribution for the stew pot?"

"It may be. Where did he get that bag of huckleberries?"

"He had them when we found him."

Sindak seemed to be listening to the melody of birdsong that filled the trees. Finally, he said, "What good would it do to poison the boy unless we knew she'd done it?"

Towa frowned. "Are you saying that she let the boy go and told him to walk down the riverbank, knowing that we'd find him?"

"Not necessarily us, but whoever is after her. She must know she's being followed. This way, her pursuers would find him and after hearing Toksus's story, they would be a lot more hesitant to continue pursuing—"

"Toksus!" Wakdanek shook the boy again. Toksus's body flopped like a soaked corn-husk doll in the Healer's muscular arms. For a protracted interval the light seeped from Toksus's eyes until he stared vacantly at the afternoon sky.

"Is he dead?" Hehaka demanded to know. His batlike face contorted.

Odion walked over to him and said, "It wasn't your fault, Hehaka. He'd been witched."

Wakdanek clutched the child to his chest and held him, but thoughts churned behind his frantic eyes. As though he was dealing with priceless statuary, the Healer placed Toksus's body on the ground and rose to his feet. His huge fists balled at his sides. He seemed to be straining against the overwhelming desire to commit murder.

"Wakdanek?" Koracoo called. "Why don't you join us? We need to talk."

It wasn't good to give men too much time to whip up their rage. It was like a dam being filled with runoff. The instant a trickle went over the edge, the flood washed away the world. *I have to force him to think.*

"Was it poison?" she asked.

The man wiped his eyes on his sleeve as he walked over to join their circle. The blend of shock and rage had left him shaking. "What did h-he tell you before I arrived?"

"You heard most of it," Koracoo said, speaking calmly and clearly. "He said Gannajero had stabbed the other boy, then forced your cousin to catch his last breath. After that she cut out the eyes—"

"Yes, I know all that, but there must have been more."

"Your cousin said that he walked all night to get here, and had to rest, and that when he awoke from his nap, he found the other boy lying beside him."

Wakdanek tilted his head and blinked as though trying to figure it out. "Someone carried the other boy here and placed him beside my cousin while he slept?"

"Apparently."

"But...who would do such a thing? And why?" Wakdanek started flexing his fists.

Koracoo glanced around at the men's faces. Sindak and Towa seemed to sense the danger. They gripped their war clubs harder and edged back slightly. Koracoo stood her ground.

"Come with me. I want to show you something. Sindak and Towa will understand immediately. I'll explain the history to you as we march back to meet Gonda and Cord."

She guided them over to the dogwoods and used CorpseEye to lift the branches so that the three men could see the tracks.

Towa sucked in a breath and dropped to his knees. "Are they the same?"

"I think so. Take a good look. I need to know if you agree with me."

Sindak fell into a crouch beside Towa, and while they discussed the herringbone sandal tracks, Koracoo rose to face Wakdanek.

"We've seen similar tracks before," she explained.

"Where?"

"Everywhere Gannajero travels."

Wakdanek frowned at the ground. "One of her *hanehwa?*"

"Skin-beings wear sandals?" Sindak asked, confused.

"They are like ghosts. They wear whatever they had on when they died," Wakdanek said. "But I—"

"It's Shagoniyoh." Odion's voice rose from right behind Koracoo.

She turned to look at her son. Odion was standing less than one pace away, sucking on his lower lip, trying to see what Sindak and Towa were doing. His shoulder-length hair dangled over one brown eye.

"Who's Shagoniyoh?" Wakdanek gently asked.

Odion wet his lips, as though he feared no one would believe him. "He helped us escape Gannajero. He's very powerful."

Tutelo said, "He's a Human False Face."

Koracoo frowned. "Why haven't you told me this before now?"

"You were busy, Mother," Odion softly replied.

Koracoo heaved a breath. She had been busy, apparently too busy to ask her own children the kind of questions that would have helped her understand what had happened to them. With as much patience as she could muster, she said, "Odion, I need to know everything that happened. Every detail."

Tutelo walked up to stand behind her brother.

"Mother, Shagoniyoh used to come visit us in Gannajero's camps. He—"

"That's true," Baji said. "I think he's a Forest Spirit that takes care of children."

"Takes care of children? Is he...?" She waved CorpseEye in frustration. "Is he a child?"

Odion shook his head. "I'm not sure what he is, Mother. Gannajero calls him The Child, but I've never gotten a good look at him. Sometimes...I think he's a—a crow. He seems to be able to fly. Other times...maybe a wolf...he runs so fast. I..."

Koracoo's expression must have reflected her disbelief. Odion closed his mouth and blinked self-consciously.

Towa stepped to Odion's side and put a hand on his shoulder. "I believe them, War Chief. When the children told us, we—"

"The children told *you?* When?"

Towa winced. "Right after we made camp in the plum grove. You and Gonda were standing guard. Tutelo heard us talking about the herringbone sandal prints, and she—"

"That's not right," Tutelo corrected him. "You were talking about how scared you were when you heard Father first call Odion's name. You said that the night you were chased by the warriors you'd heard the man wearing the herringbone sandals call Odion's name." She aimed a small hand at Towa. "Then I told Towa that it was Shagoniyoh.

Because Shagoniyoh had been calling to Odion for days. Don't you remember me saying those things?"

The air seemed to go out of Koracoo's body. She leveled lethal glares at Sindak and Towa. "She told you all of these things and you never told me?"

Sindak's shoulders hunched. "Koracoo, it's not as though we've had time to sit around the fire and have a long conversation. We told you everything we thought was really important, like the fact that Towa thought he'd seen Atotarho in the big warriors' camp, as well as—"

Wakdanek stiffened. "Atotarho? The Hills People chief? In that camp? Did his warriors attack our village, too?" His voice kept rising until it was shrill.

To ease the tension, Koracoo said, "Wakdanek, Towa *thought* he saw Atotarho there. He wasn't sure. He saw the man from a great distance. He may have been mistaken."

Wakdanek's shoulder muscles relaxed a little, but his expression remained grim. To Tutelo, he said, "What else did you tell Sindak and Towa that night?"

Tutelo glanced at Koracoo as though no longer certain who to answer. Koracoo nodded. "Continue, Tutelo."

"Well, I told Towa that Shagoniyoh was a Human False Face, and Towa pulled the shell gorget from his cape and said, 'Does he wear one of these?' That's when Hehaka woke up and said that his father used to have a gorget like that."

Wakdanek stared at Towa as though waiting to see it.

Koracoo aimed CorpseEye at Towa's chest. "Show Wakdanek the gorget."

"But, War Chief, it's not a thing for ordinary eyes! Atotarho told me never to—"

"Do it."

Grumbling, Towa reached into his shirt and pulled it out. The magnificent shell pendant covered half his chest. The hideous bent-nose False Face in the center, representing Horned Serpent, was surrounded by falling stars.

Wakdanek stared uncomfortably at the pendant. Very few people had ever seen it up close, and outsiders were never allowed to gaze upon it. Koracoo could feel the Power pulsing around the gorget. CorpseEye warmed in her hand. It was almost as though the Spirits that lived in the objects were speaking to each other in voices humans could not hear. A tingle ran up her arm.

"What does it signify?" Wakdanek whispered reverently.

Towa explained, "It chronicles the story of Horned Serpent and the destruction of the world in the Beginning Time."

Sindak stared at it in awe. The ancient pendant

told the most sacred story of all: the great battle between human beings and Horned Serpent.

"Tell me the story," Wakdanek said sharply. "The whole story."

Towa's brows drew together. "I'll tell you the part that we tell outsiders."

Wakdanek nodded.

Towa said, "At the dawn of creation, Horned Serpent crawled out of Skanodario Lake and attacked the People. His poisonous breath, like a black cloud, swept over the land, killing almost everyone. In terror, the People cried out to the Great Spirit, and he sent Thunder to help them. A vicious battle ensued, and Thunder threw the greatest lightning bolt ever seen. The flash was so bright many of the People were instantly blinded. Then the concussion struck. The mountains shook, and the stars broke loose from the skies. As they came hurtling down, they hissed right over the People. Thousands slammed into Great-Grandmother Earth. The ferocious blasts and scorching heat caused raging forest fires. The biggest star fell right into the lake on top of Horned Serpent. There was a massive explosion of steam and—as Horned Serpent thrashed his enormous tail in pain—gigantic waves coursed down the river valleys and surged over the hills in a series of colossal floods that drowned most of the People. Of the entire tribe, only five families remained—the five families who would become the Peoples that today live south of Skanodario Lake."

Sindak added, "That pendant is especially important because legend says that at the time of the cataclysm, two pendants were carved by the breath of Horned Serpent. This one has been handed down from clan matron to clan matron for generations, and now belongs to our chief. The other belongs to the Human False Face who will don a cape of white clouds and ride the winds of destruction across the face of the world in the future."

Wakdanek turned to Hehaka. "Your father had one like that?"

Hehaka's nose wiggled. "I think he was my father. I don't remember very much from before I became Gannajero's slave, but I remember that gorget. It used to swing over me when the man bent to kiss me at night." He hugged himself as though it hurt to remember. "The last time I saw it, I was four summers."

Wakdanek's brows lowered. In a menacing voice, he said, "Are you telling me your father is Atotarho?"

Hehaka looked as though he'd been struck with a club. "You—you mean my father is a chief?"

"No," Koracoo stated. "That's just one possibility."

"But who else could it be?" Wakdanek asked sharply. "Surely you're not suggesting—"

"My father is a great Hills People chief?" Hehaka blurted. An expression of almost horrified delight came over his face. His nose wiggled as he sniffed the air, clearly smelling for the gorget.

Sindak offhandedly replied, "We don't know that, Hehaka. The war chief is right. It's just as likely that your father is the Human False Face who will ride the winds of destruction."

Hehaka gasped, and Koracoo gave Sindak an annoyed look.

"It's even more likely," she said, "that there are many copies of that gorget, and your father owned one. Gonda and I found an exact copy of that gorget resting near the dead body of a girl on the border of Hills People country."

In unison, Towa and Sindak blurted, "You did?"

"What happened to it?" Wakdanek asked.

"We left it. We had no use for it."

Baji's gaze went from person to person, and she flapped her arms against her sides. "We're wasting time, War Chief. Gannajero must be just ahead of us on the river. We need to go find the other children before it's too late."

Sadness twisted Wakdanek's face and made the barely fleshed bones seem to stick out more. "I can't just leave the boys here. If wolves find them...

I can't even bear to think about it. I have to take care of them. Please, go on ahead. I'll find a way to catch up."

Sindak walked forward. "Can I help you?"

Wakdanek gave him a suspicious look, but said, "I would appreciate that."

"Very well, but we can't wait for you." Koracoo propped CorpseEye on her shoulder again. "If you're not at the canoes within one finger of time, we'll go on without you."

"Yes, go." Wakdanek waved a hand. "Sindak will be there. I'll make sure of it. And if I'm not, I'll meet you somewhere on the river."

Koracoo nodded. "All right. Towa, take the lead. Children, follow him. I'll bring up the rear."

Zateri had almost reached the camp when she heard moccasins shishing in the leaves behind her.

She turned to see Auma and Conkesema dogging her steps, threading their way between birches and maples. She shook her head and waited for them to catch up. They both had old leaves and dry grass in their hair.

"We thought you might need help," Auma explained. Her thin dress clung to her tall, slender body.

"You mean you were afraid to stay there by yourselves."

Auma had a guilty look on her face. "Well, we thought we heard warriors. It turned out to be two elk, but—"

"Just be quiet." Zateri breathed the words. "I

think the camp is abandoned, but I keep hearing something just ahead."

Auma and Conkesema went silent. The faint crackling sound came again. Zateri studied the Cloud People. They had formed a bruised blanket overhead, and the temperature was dropping. Every time she exhaled, her breath frosted before her. The only thing that kept her warm was walking.

Auma whispered, "How close are we to the camp?"

Zateri pointed and continued toward the river. She could hear the rushing water. Three people made a lot more noise than one. Leaves rattled. Twigs cracked. She heartily wished they'd stayed behind. She could stand being recaptured, but she couldn't bear the thought that they might be. They had not yet seen the extent of Gannajero's cruelty. More than almost anything, she wanted to spare them that. When they got closer, she would force them—

"Look!" Auma hissed, and pointed. "In the tree. What...what is that?"

Only slowly did Zateri become aware of the thing floating in the maple. It appeared in the deepest shadows, then fluttered into view. It looked vaguely human, and wore a shimmering translucent material. As she squinted, it seemed to be flying, rising upon each icy gust, then falling down only to rise again.

"Blessed Spirits," Auma hissed. "It's a ghost!"

Zateri had never seen a homeless ghost before, though she knew they roamed the forest, along with other kinds of Spirit beings. Fear warmed her veins.

"Maybe. Let's get closer."

"Are you mad? I just told you it's a *ghost!* I'm not getting closer to it!" Auma said.

Zateri wound through the underbrush until she could see it swaying in the maple branches. A rectangular frame lay canted at an angle in the brush below, but she had no idea what it was.

When the Cloud People parted and sunlight streaked across the heavens, the ghost became even more fantastic. It was nearly transparent, but it crackled as it floated up and down. The kind of crackle that made the breath still in Zateri's lungs.

Then something miraculous happened. The wind shifted, and flashes of color appeared and disappeared. The ghost held a prism, a rainbow, in its heart. The ground beneath it glistened with wings of light.

"Oh, gods, no." Frantically, she began searching the forest floor, thrashing through the underbrush until she saw the body.

Carefully, Zateri picked her way around old

stumps and brush to reach it. She had to clench her hands to still them.

The old woman is a monster.

"What is it?" Auma murmured as she worked through the brush to get to Zateri.

"It's a body," Zateri said. "He's been skinned."

Dark red flesh covered the bones and looked startling against the white teeth in the gaping mouth.

Conkesema trotted up behind Auma. When she saw the body, her mouth opened, but no words came out—only a single note, soft and sweet, like the beginning of a phoebe's song. The purity was stunning. It went on and on, then abruptly rose to a breathless shriek.

"No, Conkesema!" Auma leaped for her and put a hand over her mouth.

The little girl fought like a wildcat, tearing at Auma's hands, struggling to run away. Auma clamped her lips against Conkesema's ear and snarled, "Stop it. *Stop!* They'll hear us. They'll come!"

Conkesema sagged in her arms, sobbing. Auma stroked her hair. "It's all right. Just don't cry. Don't cry."

Zateri moved into the clearing and bravely walked beneath the ghost. Rainbows danced upon her upturned face. "It's the skin. A dried human skin. It must have been stretched over the frame, but the frame fell off when the wind—"

"Who is it?" Auma released Conkesema, and the girl sank to the ground and covered her face with her dress hem. Auma walked to stand beside Zateri. "Is it Wrass?"

"The corpse is too big. It's probably that guard Akio. This was his punishment for letting us escape. She turned him into one of her *hanehwa*."

Zateri studied the ground. The leaves were thick in this small clearing, and Wind Mother had stirred them around. There were no tracks, no trails. But Gannajero's men must have walked back to the river where the canoes were stowed.

She carefully made her way down to the shore and frowned. Near one of the places where they'd shoved off, there were strange drag marks.

"What's this?" she said just above a whisper.

"Did you find something?"

"Yes, but I'm not sure what it is."

Zateri knelt. When her eyes narrowed, the reflections off the water seemed to grow brighter. "One of them must have been hurt. I see handprints beside the drag marks, but no footprints. The handprints are small."

"A boy's?"

Hope was rushing in her veins. She put her fingers over one of the handprints. It was only slightly larger than hers. "Yes," the soft cry erupted from her lips before she knew it. "I—I think it's Wrass."

Auma hurried over to look. "He escaped?"

Zateri sank down on the sand to look at the handprints more closely. Something was wrong. A frightening sensation constricted her chest, squeezing it until she couldn't breathe. "Auma, if he's dragging himself, he's hurt badly."

"Maybe that's why the old woman left him. He was dying." The words were like a deerbone stiletto in Zateri's heart. She longed to strike the girl. But she got to her feet and let her gaze follow the drag marks up the shore. He couldn't have gone far. "I'm going to find him."

6

Sonon leaned against the trunk of a hemlock and watched the snow fall out of the lingering blue dusk. The storm had quieted the forest and given it a luminous serenity. Even the sound of the nearby river seemed hushed.

He tipped his face up and let the cold flakes land on his skin. The boys whispered to his right. He didn't look at them, but knew they sat atop the rounded humps where Wakdanek and Sindak had buried them less than one hand of time ago.

He closed his eyes and just tried to feel.

One of the boys laughed, and it filled his tired heart with warmth. As long as Wakdanek lived, they'd be all right. The Healer would come back and make sure they got home to their families, who would in turn make sure they were properly prepared to cross the bridge to the afterlife.

He shoved away from the tree and turned toward the river. In the subdued light the water had a leaden sheen.

He wasn't needed here.

He headed south down the shore.

Nothing mattered now except his steps; they would decide everything. Steps always did. A man might plan for every detail and try to prepare himself for all the things that could go wrong, but in the end steps were all that mattered. Steps created the path. Steps brought you to the final moment when you had to stand face-to-face with all the grief you'd ever been asked to shelter in your heart. Your own, as well as that of others. It didn't matter who you were, or how you'd lived...the enormity was unbearable. It slammed you down. When you struggled up again, the grief either transformed into the Healer's balm or it became a murderer's inspiration.

He concentrated on placing one foot in front of the other.

Somewhere just ahead, he would take the final steps.

7

Only the muffled tramping of their feet on snow-covered leaves filled the twilight.

"We'll have to stop soon," Auma said from behind her. "It's getting too dark to see the drag marks, and the snow is falling harder."

Zateri didn't answer. Panic was running hot and fierce in her body. She couldn't believe Wrass had dragged himself this far, but she knew him. The darkness and snow wouldn't stop him. He'd keep moving, trying to put distance between himself and Gannajero, until he was physically unable to continue and collapsed in death.. If she didn't find him soon, she never would. The snow would fill the drag marks, and his trail would be erased from the world.

"Did you hear me?" Auma asked. "We should stop for the night."

"I'm not stopping." Zateri kept her gaze on the ground. A shallow swale marked the path where Wrass had dragged himself through the falling snow. It led around a thicket of willows and up into the trees. As she walked along beside the swale, gigantic flakes swirled around her, landing cold and silent on her hood and cape.

"*Zateri!* We have to stop!"

She swung around with her jaw locked. She was too exhausted and frightened to tolerate weakness. In anyone. "If you can't keep up, then sit down. I'll come back for you as soon as I find Wrass."

Auma clutched the collar of her doehide dress closed beneath her chin. "I wasn't trying to make you angry. We're tired and hungry. We can barely see. I—"

"Stop complaining. I can't stand it. Don't you think I'm tired and hungry, too?"

Zateri glared at her and turned back to the trail.

She followed his path around a massive sycamore trunk, then down a slope. Auma and Conkesema resolutely plodded along behind her.

Zateri's taut nerves hummed. Every noise, even the whisper of an owl's wings overhead, left her shaking. She loved the woods at home, but this forest lay as though under some dread enchantment. She could sense Forest Spirits moving around her, tracking her through the haunted darkness, peering at her between the frosted branches. Every now and then, she glimpsed something blacker than the shadows drifting through the trees. And there was more than one.

But she couldn't let fear stop her. Auma was right about one thing: the light was almost gone. Time was running out.

Ahead of her loomed the dark bulk of a toppled maple. The roots thrust up into the air like crooked arms. Straining her eyes against the falling flakes, she thought the trail led toward it.

Her moccasins squealed in the snow as she trudged ahead. In the hollow beneath the upturned roots, there was a dark splotch, a mound, like an animal curled on its...

"Wrass?" she cried. Down the swale she ran, slipping across the snow, her cape streaming behind her. "Wrass? *Wrass!*"

He woke with a start and shoved up on his elbows. Weakly, he answered, "Zateri?"

"Thank the gods we found you."

She launched herself at him, but the instant her arms went around him, her joy vanished. Earlier in the day, the snow must have melted on his cape as he'd dragged himself, soaking it. He was cold to the bone...but he wasn't shivering. She pushed away and stared at him. He was wobbling, and his eyes had a dreamy half-awake look, as though he wasn't sure she was real.

"Zateri?" he said again in a faint voice.

She spun around in panic. "He's freezing to death. Gather wood. We have to warm him up."

Auma wrung her hands. "But...won't Ganna-jero see the fire?"

"Get wood *now!*"

Auma and Conkesema scrambled through the falling snow, breaking off the dead branches at the bases of the trees. They would be the driest wood around. In the meantime, Zateri pulled Wrass' wet cape over his head and draped it across two roots to serve as a kind of roof over his head. Then she pulled off her own cape and slipped it around him. As she tugged it down over his arms, he blinked up at her. Snowflakes coated his narrow face and perched upon his hooked nose.

"Zateri." As he said her name, tears filled his eyes. "I hurt...my ankle. Can't walk."

"I'll take care of it, I promise. For now, I need you to stay awake."

"But I'm so t-tired."

She grabbed him by the shoulders and stared at him. "I don't care how tired you are. Stay awake or I'll beat you with a stick. Do you hear me?"

His head wobbled, but a smile came to his lips. "You really are here. I...I wasn't sure. Been s-seeing things. Faces...in the forest."

Auma and Conkesema returned, piled wood beside Zateri, and went back for more.

As Zateri started digging a hole in the snow to create a pit for the fire, she said, "Yes, I'm really here, and I'm going to take care of you, Wrass. You're going to be all right."

But as she arranged the kindling in the pit, she kept glancing out at the dark forest.

8

A gloating smile curled Gannajero's toothless mouth. All around her, her men crouched in the brush or stood behind tree trunks. In the falling snow, they blended perfectly with the forest shadows. She couldn't even hear them breathing.

For Kotin's ears alone, she said, "I told you Chipmunk Teeth would never leave the boy. Order our men to slowly spread out. I don't want any mistakes this time."

9

The evening breeze was freezing cold and carried the distant howling of wolves.

"Tree." Koracoo leaned out of the bow to point.

Cord moved trancelike, dipped his oar, and steered the canoe around the snag that bobbed along in the water. The snow was falling so heavily he could barely see the spinning branches. If they struck something like this in the darkness, it would rip the bottom right off the birch-bark canoe. But he wasn't about to be the one to suggest to Koracoo that they stop for the night. For the past hand of time, she'd been terse, concentrating on the river.

Cord dipped his paddle again. Waves spun away, colliding with the whitecaps and leaves floating on the muddy surface. Somewhere upstream, the storm must have been violent.

Debris, including whole trees, had washed into the Quill River.

Sindak, who sat in the stern just behind Cord, murmured, "She's going to get us killed."

"We can still see. We're all right."

"What makes you think she'll stop when we can't see?"

Sindak's snow-covered hood shielded most of his face, but Cord could see one of his eyes and his beaked nose. Uneasy, Cord asked, "Have you ever seen her canoe through a blizzard at night?"

"No, but this isn't any ordinary night, is it? She knows we're close. There's no telling what she'll—"

"If you're trying to be secretive," Koracoo said from the bow, "your voices are not nearly low enough."

She turned to stare at them over her shoulder. Some time ago, she'd shoved her hood back so she could see better, and her short hair stuck wetly to her face. "Stop complaining."

Sindak called, "I just thought I should tell you that I can no longer see my paddle."

She just dipped her oar again.

Odion glanced back and forth between them. He sat in the middle of the canoe with his puppy asleep in his lap. He'd barely let the wolf out of his hands since Toksus' death. Atop the packs in front of Odion, Tutelo slept soundly. Long black hair haloed her pretty face. She reminded Cord a little of his daughter, and that brought him both pain and joy.

"I'm trying to tell you..." Sindak began, but halted when Koracoo suddenly pulled her oar out of the water and tugged CorpseEye from her belt. Her gaze darted over the shore.

"That's worrisome," Sindak noted.

Cord watched her for a time; then he whispered, "What's happening? I've seen her do this before. It's as though..."

"CorpseEye is speaking to her? Oh, my friend, I have seen things you would not believe."

"For example?"

"CorpseEye is old," Sindak replied, and calmly stroked the water. "He often hears or sees things that humans do not, and when he does, he tries to get Koracoo's attention."

"How?"

"She told me once that Power flows from CorpseEye into her hands. It's a warmth that can be painful."

As he said the words, Koracoo shifted CorpseEye to her other hand and scanned the trees on the eastern bank as though deeply worried.

Sindak said, "There must be something out there."

"Something good? Something bad? Is CorpseEye warning her?"

Sindak shook his head, and snow caked off his

hood and piled on his shoulders. "The last time I saw this, we had completely lost the children's trail. We were desperate, biting each other's heads off. CorpseEye led us to the trail again. Good? Bad? We'll find out."

"Curious," Cord murmured.

Every warrior breathed Spirit into his weapons, and knew they were alive. For that reason, they were cared for and treated with respect. In the worst of times, the weapon's soul might save the warrior. But CorpseEye was different. He'd been around for so many generations that warriors for two moons' run in any direction knew the club's reputation. It was rumored that CorpseEye could kill even when it was not being wielded by its owner. Just looking at the ancient weapon with lust or greed in your heart was said to bring death.

Cord had known many shamans who possessed great Spirit objects. Usually it was a carved mask, or a stone fetish, maybe a tortoiseshell rattle. Once he'd seen an old woman who carried a turkey tail fan that she claimed cured illness. But very few weapons were endowed with such Spirit power. That's what made CorpseEye the subject of legends.

Koracoo shifted to face the eastern shore, and her forehead lined.

Cord called, "What's wrong, War Chief?"

She didn't answer. Instead, she lifted a hand

and waved them toward the shore. "We're stopping for the night. Sindak, call back to Gonda, and make sure he hears you."

As Cord dragged his paddle, turning them toward the bank, Sindak cupped a hand to his mouth and shouted, "Gonda? We're putting ashore!"

From the torrent of snow, Gonda answered, "We see you."

When they neared the bank, the swift current jostled the canoe, sending it bucking and splashing through the waves until they got close enough that Koracoo could jump into the shallows and guide the bow onto the sand.

"Keep your eyes on the trees," Cord said. "My stomach muscles just went tight."

Sindak's eyes narrowed. He stowed his paddle in the stern and nodded. "Yes, War Chief."

Koracoo reached into the canoe to collect her weapons, and while she slipped on her quiver and slung her bow, her eyes continuously scanned the towering trees.

The underbrush was especially thick here. Willows and maple saplings crowded against each other. No clear trail could be seen through the thicket. And if the animals couldn't penetrate it, could a human? Still, Cord felt uneasy. There might be warriors hiding in that dense under-growth, and they'd never see them until too late to get to the canoes. To make matters worse, there was nowhere to run except down the thin skirt of sand that lined the water.

"Mother?" Odion called. "Can I get out?"

She studied the forest for a long time before she answered, "Yes, but try not to wake Tutelo—and I want you to stay close to the canoe."

"Yes, Mother."

Odion picked up the heavy puppy and carefully climbed around his sister to leap ashore. Sindak grabbed his war club and followed the boy.

Cord remained in the canoe, gathering his weapons. He slung his quiver and bow over his left shoulder, checked to make sure his stilettos and knife were tied on his belt, then clutched his war club. As he started forward, Gonda's canoe came slapping across the waves, and the man called, "Sindak? Give us a hand."

Sindak trotted over and waited for the canoe to come in close enough that he could grab the bow and drag it onto the bank while Wakdanek and Towa paddled hard to keep the boat from being dragged back out into the current.

Gonda wasted no time. He seemed to sense something was amiss. He picked up every weapon he owned and strapped it on, then leaped ashore and stalked toward Koracoo. He said something to her that Cord didn't hear. She nodded and replied, "CorpseEye...this grove of maples."

Baji and Hehaka scrambled ashore behind Gonda and whispered to each other.

An eerie sensation of impending doom prickled Cord's spine. He stepped silently around the sleeping Tutelo, braced a hand on the gunwale, and vaulted to the sand. He walked to join Sindak and Towa.

As the three of them stood in the falling snow, Towa said, "Did CorpseEye lead us here?"

"Yes," Sindak replied. "How did you know?"

Towa pulled his hood forward to shield his face from the storm. "This is a bad place to camp. Koracoo wouldn't have chosen it."

"You think her club is brainless? Or just a bad judge of campsites?"

"I think CorpseEye couldn't care less about our safety or comfort. He has other priorities."

"What other priorities?" Cord asked.

The two warriors had been with Koracoo and Gonda for about a moon. They knew far more about the war chief's weapon than Cord did.

Sindak's eyes lifted to the trees, searching the limbs. "I wouldn't be too eager to find out, if I were you."

Towa shivered and rubbed his arms. "It's going to be a freezing night. We should collect wood before it gets too dark to see."

Cord used his club to point to a copse of elms. At some time in the past, they'd been attacked by worms. Half the branches were dead. "Those will be the driest branches."

Sindak's breath frosted when he answered, "Towa and I will do it."

Willow stems clattered as Sindak and Towa shoved through them to get to the dead branches. For a time, Cord let them work while he scrutinized the area. The snowfall was still steady, but it had slowed down. About half as many flakes whirled from the sky.

He glimpsed movement to his left, and turned to see Odion and Gitchi walking along the sand toward him. The boy had a moonish face, with soft brown eyes. Inside his hood, Odion's shoulder-length hair clung wetly to his jaw. The young wolf trotted happily at his side with his tongue hanging out.

As he approached, Odion said, "Mother told me I could walk down the shore so long as I keep you in sight."

Cord nodded. "Very well, but as soon as we've gathered wood we'll be walking back."

"I won't go far."

"Make sure you don't."

Odion nodded and continued down the shore with Gitchi bouncing along at his heels.

Cord took one final look at the forest and river; then he waded through the brush to help Sindak and Towa collect wood.

10
ODION

A faint pewter gleam lingers as I walk down the shore through the falling snow. Twilight is rapidly giving way to night. Gitchi lopes at my side. The strip of sand is very narrow here, bordered on my right by the wide river and on my left by thick brush. Beyond the brush, trees rattle as Wind Mother blows the storm across the forest.

I step wide around a big rock, taller than I am, that is lodged in the middle of the sand. It narrows the path until it's just barely wide enough to edge by without stepping in the water. As I slide past, Gitchi splashes through the river, swerves around the rock, and trots ahead into the darkness.

"Gitchi, wait! Don't get too far ahead. Come here, boy."

I find him on the other side. He's standing with one wet paw lifted, staring to the south, sniffing the air. The dim gleam of evening makes him look like a ghost dog. He is a dove-colored phantom wavering in and out of the falling snow.

A low growl rumbles in his throat.

"What's wrong, boy?"

Gitchi scents the wind again and turns to me expectantly.

Wind Mother is blowing up from the south, swirling snow around and thrashing through the brush. I turn to face into the wind and my eyes widen. "That's smoke."

A campfire? A village?

Fear twists my stomach as I back away. "Come on, Gitchi. We're going back right now."

His ears prick, and he trots to me with his bushy tail wagging. I reach down and stroke his silken head. "Good boy. Thanks for warning me."

My moccasins crunch in the snow as I head for the rock. Just before I edge around it, Wind Mother's howling dies down, and the river's hushed roar seems louder. I tip my head back to look up into the falling flakes. They are half the size of my palm and silently spiral down to melt on my face. When I lick them from my lips, they have a clean earthy flavor. I turn back to the trail.

It's grown so dark that without the snow on the path, I'm not sure I'd be able to tell where the water began and the shore—

Voices.

Behind me.

Gitchi growls, and my heart thunders.

Ahead, I hear War Chief Cord speaking with Sindak and Towa, but this is something else. I'm *sure* it came from behind me, to the south.

I concentrate on listening. I don't hear anything now, but fear is burning up from my belly into my chest and filtering out to my fingertips. It is as though my soul hears the voice even if my ears don't.

Gitchi must smell or sense my panic. He goes as quiet and still as the dead, but his yellow eyes peer intently at the night, searching for the threat.

I swear there's something there, just below my ability to hear. And it's *familiar*.

I close my eyes and try to separate the human tones from the burbling of the river, the clattering of branches, and Sindak's voice. My head rotates, searching, moving toward the southeast. When I open my eyes, I am stunned. Fifty paces away, a fluttering orange gleam dances through the forest. It was probably there all along; I just couldn't see it through the snowfall.

That voice again.

The notes are sweet and high. A girl's voice.

I clench my fists and whisper, "Zateri?"

As I walk toward the voice, Gitchi whimpers, trying to tell me there is danger ahead, but I can't stop myself. The need to know is overwhelming.

The brush fades into tree trunks the size of three

men standing together. Against the slate gray of night, the thick limbs trace crooked black lines. As the snow falls, the flakes pick up the orange gleam and glisten like embers floating down.

Gitchi lays his ears back, and his tail sticks straight out behind him. His gaze rivets on the flickering firelight. His steps are utterly silent. He can tell from my stealthy movements that we're hunting, and he's spotted the prey. He knows silence is of the utmost importance now.

When I stand ten paces away, flame-shadows gyrate, turning the frosted branches into liquid amber.

The girl cries, "Let me go!"

Desperation makes me sick to my stomach. I edge forward another two steps. I'm breathing hard. I suck in a breath, and her name comes out like a sob, *"Zateri?"*

I stand trembling, waiting for—

Gitchi barks suddenly and leaps at something. I spin around in time to see the puppy clamp his teeth around a man's arm and start snarling and ripping, his paws scratching the ground for purchase in the slippery snow. The man wears his black hair in a bun at the back of his head and carries a war club.

"Filthy cur," the man says as he clubs Gitchi, and the puppy falls into the snow with his legs twitching. A desperate whine escapes Gitchi's bloody jaws.

"No!" I run forward. When I fall into the snow beside him, Gitchi looks up at me pleadingly. Blood pours from his head wound. I reach to pick him up, but the man grabs my arm, drags me to my feet, and clamps a hand over my mouth. In my ear, he whispers, "How many people are with you? Nod your head for each one."

I will not. I claw at his fingers. He's pressing so hard my teeth are cutting into my lower lip. Blood wells in my mouth.

"You're a little warrior, eh? Well, don't worry, we'll beat that out of you."

The man half drags me to a deer trail that winds through the trunks toward the fire. Many people have walked this trail recently. The snow has been trampled, leaving a black slash through the white.

As he shoves me into a small clearing, a cry climbs my throat. A boy is huddled before the fire, rocking back and forth, shivering hard.

Against the man's hand, I try to scream his name, but only a garbled sound vibrates in my throat.

The man's breath is fetid as he bends down to hiss in my face, "Make a sound and my men will kill your entire party."

I nod, and as he slowly removes his hand, I wipe blood from my lips with my sleeve. My knees have gone wobbly. *"Wrass?"*

He turns, and I see the tears on his cheeks. He looks utterly broken. He's shivering so hard he can't seem to keep his eyes on me, but his shaking voice is clear. "S-sorry, Odion. So s-sorry."

The man shoves me hard, and I careen toward the fire. "Sit down, and stay quiet."

I drop to my knees beside Wrass, and he whispers, "They l-let me go…knew I'd…lead them…to the others."

"Others?" I whisper in sudden terror. "What others? I thought I heard—"

"Close your mouths," the man orders, and swings his war club to emphasize his words.

I stare at him, but Wrass's head falls forward, and he starts sobbing as though his heart is breaking.

11

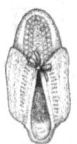

W hat was that?" Cord stared southward. "Did you hear that? I thought I heard a boy's voice."

Sindak cracked off another branch, placed it in the crook of his left arm, and replied, "I heard something, but I don't know what it was."

Towa's handsome face tightened. "It sounded like a dog's bark to me. Where's Odion?"

Cord dumped his armload of wood and pulled his war club from his belt. "This could be nothing, but get back to camp. Tell War Chief Koracoo that if I'm not there with Odion in five hundred heartbeats, something is wrong."

Cord didn't wait to see if they obeyed him; he trotted down the shore.

The clouds had parted. Moonlight slanted across the snowy forest in bars and streaks. Where it touched, the ground gleamed as though coated with silver dust.

Cord slid around the boulder that blocked the path and heard a pathetic whimper. He eased his head out and peered at the trail. Almost invisible in the moonlight, the young wolf was dragging himself along Odion's footprints, whimpering and struggling, trying to get to the place in the forest where firelight flickered.

Hot blood surged through Cord's veins.

A warriors' camp? No. If a warrior had clubbed a puppy, he would have already spitted him and had him roasting over the flames. The man who clubbed Gitchi didn't have the luxury of picking him up. He needed both hands, one for his weapon and one for Odion.

Cord surveyed the grove of maples and sycamores, then slowly made his way to the puppy and kneeled down. As Cord petted him, Gitchi's tail weakly thumped the ground. "Were you trying to get to him, to protect him?" Cord asked softly. "You're a brave boy."

Gitchi whined.

"Don't worry. I'm coming back for you."

Cord silently rose and started for the orange halo of firelight.

Odion's footprints marked the way.

12

ODION

The man turns away from us to scan the forest, and I whisper, "Wrass, we're going to get out of here. I'm not alone. Just down the shore—"

"Shh!" Wrass hisses, and glances at the warrior.

As though I'm trying to help keep my friend warm, I put my arm around Wrass's shoulder and draw him close while I whisper in his ear, "Where's the rest of the war party? I don't see them."

His chin subtly tips toward the forest to my left, then indicates other places. I can't force myself to look. I'm too afraid of what I'll see. "How many?"

He shakes his head as though he doesn't know for sure. This isn't like Wrass. He is a warrior. He always knows who and what he is facing. Has the cold taken his senses? There is a woodpile beside the fire. I grasp a branch and lay it on the flames. As the fire eats through the bark, it crackles, and sparks flit toward the limbs above.

Wrass has his head bowed to hide the movements of his mouth. "The old w-woman hired more men. Don't know how many."

13

From where Koracoo stood guard beneath the leafless maple branches at the edge of the clearing, she could see Gonda and Wakdanek adding twigs to the fire, preparing it for the larger branches that Cord's wood-gathering party would bring. Already a weak amber gleam flickered through the trees and reflected from the river. Tutelo and Hehaka crouched before the tiny blaze with their hands extended. Both were shivering. Their soft voices seemed to echo in the snowfall and increased the deep sense of unease that tormented her.

CorpseEye was warm against her fingers, telling her there was something out there. She spread her feet and gripped the ancient club in tight fists, preparing herself for the worst.

Gonda called, "What's keeping Cord? We could use that wood now."

Wakdanek replied, "Why don't I take the children and collect some more of the driftwood along the shore? We'll add it to the pile. That should be enough to keep the blaze going until—"

"Quiet!" Koracoo stiffened at the sound of feet pounding up from the south, coming hard along the shore. "Gonda?"

He was instantly on his feet, his club in his hand. From many summers of warring together, he had learned every possible tone in her voice, and he knew this was more than just Cord returning from wood gathering.

"Where?" he softly asked.

She tipped her chin to the south.

Wakdanek rose to his feet and pulled his club from his belt. "It's probably just Cord, or Sindak and Towa."

Gonda turned to the children. "Baji, take Tutelo and Hehaka. Get in the canoe. Hide yourselves under the packs."

Baji didn't ask a single question. She scrambled to her feet and led the other children to the canoes. As they pulled packs over the top of them, Gonda said, "Wakdanek, if anything happens, I want you in that canoe and headed down the river with the children. If we're able, we'll catch you before dawn.

If we haven't caught you by then, don't stop. Do you understand?"

Wakdanek swallowed hard and nodded. "I do."

As the steps pounded closer, Koracoo silently slipped behind the maple trunk and shifted CorpseEye for an easy swing at the first man's head.

Most of the storm had passed, though Cloud People still filled the heavens and cast dark shadows as they journeyed northward, apparently following the river. Snow fell lightly, obscuring Koracoo's view. She stared hard at the moonlit trail...and made out Sindak, coming fast. There was only one man behind him. Towa. She could tell from the way he moved.

As he ran for the clearing, she called, "Where's Cord? Where's my son?"

Sindak stumbled when she stepped out from behind the maple and onto the trail in front of him. "Odion," he said, breathing hard. "We heard a shout and a bark. Cord went to find him. It's probably nothing, but Cord said that if he wasn't back in five hundred heartbeats, you should—"

Sindak's voice faded as his eyes lifted and rapidly darted over the trees around the clearing. He said only, "War Chief."

"Koracoo?" Gonda called almost simultaneously.

She turned to see faces gleaming in the faint

light cast by the fire. They stood behind trees, but she could see their drawn bows. The fletching on the arrows shimmered.

"Lay down your weapons," a man called from the shadows. "We have you surrounded. If you don't do as I say, we'll capture the children and make you watch while we gut them."

Every eye turned to Koracoo. Gonda was gritting his teeth, glaring in disgust that they'd allowed themselves to be cornered like this. Wakdanek's face had gone stony.

"Do as he says." Koracoo gently placed CorpseEye on a snow-covered pile of old leaves. As she slipped her bow and quiver from her shoulder and placed them beside CorpseEye, she whispered to Sindak, "I count eight. You?"

"Eight," he replied, "maybe nine. I think there's someone standing at the edge of the firelight to the north." She heard snow crunch as he and Towa placed their clubs within reach.

Towa added, "And two behind us, War Chief, blocking the trail."

"Our only escape route," Sindak said in a vaguely annoyed voice. "They've been watching and assessing us for a long time. Probably since we landed. Their camp must be nearby."

Koracoo glanced at CorpseEye. He had never led her into a trap before. There had to be more here than she was seeing.

A tall man with broken yellow teeth stepped out of the forest and walked into the firelight. He moved like a gangly stork wading the shallows and wore a beautiful red leather cape trimmed with seashells.

More warriors emerged from the trees, spreading out, circling them like a pack of hungry wolves. Each carried a drawn bow, and several of them were warriors from the People Who Separated. She could tell from their hats, made from the shoulder skin of a moose, which were very similar to the one Wakdanek wore. Her brows drew together as she tried to figure it out. The People Who Separated did not ally themselves with any outsiders, but the red-caped man's accent marked him as a man of the Mountain People, and she suspected by the distinctive way he moved that the skinny man to Red Cape's right was from the Landing People.

Eight men in the clearing. But Sindak was right. There was another shadow at the edge of the firelight to the north. It swayed slightly as though watching the proceedings, merely observing. And there could be many more out in the trees.

"I am Kotin," Red Cape greeted. "Messenger for the powerful—"

"Kotin!" The cry came from the canoe. Packs scattered as Hehaka leaped to his feet and scurried across the boat to get out. He charged headlong for the man, calling, "I'm here! I'm right here. I knew you'd come for me!"

As Hehaka raced by Gonda, he grabbed the boy, swung him into his arms, and held him like a shield over his chest. "You're not going anywhere."

"Let me go!" Hehaka pounded his fists into Gonda's shoulders. "They've come for me. I have to go to them!"

Kotin lunged toward Gonda, and Gonda shouted, "Come one step closer, and I'll snap his neck."

Kotin stopped dead in his tracks. "That would be very foolish. A short distance away, we're holding two Yellowtail Village children as hostages, your son and a hawk-faced boy named Wrass. Do you want to see them dead?"

A weightless sensation possessed Koracoo as the horrifying realization sank in that they had not accidentally stumbled upon a war party, but fallen into a trap.

Gonda turned just barely toward her, and she saw the same stunned knowledge on his face. He called, "Koracoo, I assume you're going to negotiate with this piece of filth."

She started forward, and Sindak said, "I'll be right behind you."

"No," she replied. "I want you and Towa to stay out of the clearing for as long as they let you.

Be ready to grab your weapons when the fight starts."

"The sooner the better."

The men who formed the circle at the edge of the trees shifted as Koracoo walked toward Gonda, altering their aims to follow her. Her souls were doing a mad dance, calculating strategy, trying to find some way...

Kotin didn't mention Cord. If they'd captured a Flint war chief, Kotin would have boasted about it.

As she made her way into the firelight, her glance searched the shadows, praying he was out there watching this, waiting for his chance.

14

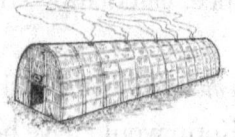

C ord silently eased through the moonlit trees east of the campfire. He'd followed Odion's path to the place where the boy had been captured, studied the two sets of tracks, then backed away and taken the long way around. After he'd followed the river south for a few hundred heartbeats, he'd circled back to the east to approach the fire through the woods rather than the noisy brush. A dense stand of maples surrounded him. The bed of moldering leaves that covered the forest floor was damp and quiet to walk upon.

He slipped from behind the trunk where he'd been hiding and moved to the next. The earthiness of freshly fallen snow suffused the air. From his new position, he could see the low fire built in the hollow beneath the uprooted tree. It cast reflections upon the long, crooked roots. But he saw no one sitting around the flames.

Was the fire a lure, meant to draw in the enemy? He suspected that the first man to walk into the light would find an arrow through his heart.

Somewhere close by, one or two warriors would be watching the fire. Where?

Dark shapes covered the ground; most of them were bushes, or saplings, but a few might be hunching men. His gaze lingered on those shapes, searching for movement. Even the most diligent warrior moved on occasion, adjusting his cape, shifting his weapons, drinking from his water bag. Unless of course, he knew he was being watched; then he froze. But in that case, Cord would already be dead.

Down the incline near the place where Odion had been captured, a vague ripple touched the darkness, like a voluminous coal black cape whipping in the wind. When the figure moved toward Cord, floating across the snow as though weightless, Cord's fist went tight around his war club.

Black Cape moved into the trees and seemed to hover between the tree trunks as though examining the tracks that led to the fire.

Cord hesitated. He had his bow and quiver. He

could have easily shot the man, but...he wasn't sure what he was seeing. A man, for certain, but he moved with an almost eerie grace. Barely a whisper of his cape disturbed the stillness as the figure glided behind the trees and continued at a leisurely pace up the hill to the northeast, starting and stopping often enough to convince Cord he was following a trail.

Cord remained perfectly still, watching until the man disappeared over the low hill.

Then Cord faded back across the leaf mat to the shadowy well behind a maple trunk and waited, listening. His four summers as a war chief, and ten summers as a warrior before that, had trained him well. He could smell peril; the forest stank of it. The silver brightness of the moonlight winking from the snow made the stillness all the more ominous. But he had the odd sense that this man was not the source of it. Something else was out here with them, and it breathed the darkness like a hunting bear.

Keeping to the tangle of shadows that weaved latticelike through the moonlight, he softly crept along behind the man, who seemed completely unaware of Cord's presence. His black cape swung when he looked down.

Cord eased behind a sycamore.

The man never turned. He kept walking straight north, paralleling the river.

Conscious of the weight of his body, Cord moved a few steps, then halted, careful not to snap twigs buried beneath the leaf mat. By angling his head, he could see through the dense trunks to a moonlit meadow ahead. The man appeared to be heading for it.

He followed.

Long before he reached the meadow, Cord was aware of the sound of children's soft voices. The hair at the nape of his neck stood up. As he crossed the ice-skimmed leaves, silvered by the night, he felt something. No sound accompanied it, no smell. It seemed to drift around him in the cold air. He shivered, trying to shake it off, but the sensation grew stronger, until it was almost overpowering. He didn't know how to explain it...it was a...a hunger, a hatred that would outlive the passing of centuries, a need for vengeance that went far beyond his comprehension.

But it called to his warrior's blood like the singing of a thousand bows fired at once.

Blood started to pound in his ears. He blinked and looked around. Black Cape had vanished. Cord hadn't even seen him move. He'd thought the man was still standing, looking down at the meadow, but...

A child sobbed.

As though the girl was buried beneath a pile of leaves ten hands deep, the sound was muffled.

Cord set his jaw and continued on down the trail that curved through the dogwoods. Just as he veered around a clump of brush...Black Cape stepped from behind a tree less than five paces away. Cord froze.

The man's ability for stillness was unnatural. Eerie. Black hair hung like silken strands around his oval, bent-nosed face. Fine as cobwebs, it shone brilliantly in the moonlight. His eyes were black as eternal night, with a wolflike luminosity. Cord couldn't take his gaze from that strangely pale face. The man's pallor contrasted so sharply with his black cape that he more resembled a corpse than a living man. And stranger still, he carried no weapons—at least none that Cord could see.

Barely above a whisper, Cord said, "Who are you?"

"One of the condemned. But no threat to you, my friend."

Cord hadn't seen his mouth move, but perhaps he'd just missed it.

"You have a Hills People accent, but you're not one of them or you wouldn't be out here alone tracking them. What—?"

"If you're going to help your friends, you'll have to hurry. They're surrounded."

"Surrounded..." A chill sensation of terror went through Cord.

"And outnumbered almost three to one. Go. *Now.*"

Before his souls had even thought it through, Cord was backing away, then running across the snow, headed back for the river camp.

15
ODION

When we finally reach the clearing, tears are streaming down Wrass' face. I have his arm stretched across my shoulders, supporting him as we fight our way through the snow. I'm practically carrying him now. He won't say it, but I know the pain in his injured ankle is very bad. He can't put any weight on it, and I keep losing my sweaty grip on his hand and stumbling to stay on my feet, which causes him even more pain.

"Keep moving," Dakion orders. "It's not much farther."

"We'd be moving faster if you'd help me carry him."

Dakion sneers. "Complain one more time, boy, and I'll lighten your load for good." He swings his war club in case I missed his meaning and adds, "Your friend is a troublemaker. We should have killed him long ago. Don't give me an excuse."

Wrass whispers, "I'm s-sorry, Odion. I wish I—"

"Save your strength, Wrass. There's a fight coming."

He gives me a sidelong look, as though he can tell I'm secretly trying to warn him that we're going to make a break for it. Wrass' expression goes sober. He knows he can't run and must be trying to figure out what I have planned.

I'm not sure myself, except that I will not become the old woman's slave again. I'll die first.

"There," Dakion says, and points to a small clearing just over the low hill. "That's where you're going."

I take a new grip on Wrass' damp hand and haul him another five paces before I have to stop and catch my breath. Ahead, I see one guard standing over two children. A strange longing rises in me. I want to see Zateri. To know she's all right. But as we get closer, the girls' faces shine in the moonlight. She is not here. Panic surges through me. I whisper to Wrass, "Where's Zateri?"

He winces and croaks, "They took her. Gannajero said they were going to need her."

"For what?"

"The old woman...said Zateri had to be there."

"Where? For what?"

Wrass shakes his head. He's breathing hard,

biting his lip with every step. At least he's no longer shivering. As I haul him over the hill and into the clearing, two girls leap to their feet and call, "Wrass! Wrass? Are you all right?"

The guards chuckle to each other. They find our concern for each other amusing.

When I reach the girls, I lower Wrass to the ground. He smothers the whimpers that try to escape his throat and looks at the girls. "Auma, are you all right?"

The older girl nods. "Yes, but they took Zateri."

Wrass uses both hands to adjust his ankle, stretching it straight out in front of him and heaving a deep sigh of relief. While he tries to get comfortable, the girls stare openly at me.

"Who are you?" Auma asks suspiciously. She is tall and slender, and has a broad nose and long eyelashes.

"His name is Odion," Wrass says. "He's my friend. From my village. He—"

"Wait," the older girl says. "Isn't he one of the boys you helped to escape?"

Wrass nods. "Yes."

As though horrified, she asks, "What's he doing here? Did they hunt him down and drag him back?"

Guilt fills me. The fact that some of us escaped must have given them hope, and now, seeing me here...

"She didn't hunt me down," I explain, and cast a

glance over my shoulder. The two guards have walked a short distance away and stand talking to each other. I keep my voice barely audible. "I came hunting for you with a war party. They are camped on the beach less than one-half hand of time away. I swear it."

"But...what are you doing here? Why aren't you with them?"

I square my shoulders. "Right after we made camp, I walked a short distance away and glimpsed Wrass' fire. Then I heard Zateri's voice. I had to see if they were really out there."

"But the war party will come looking for you, won't they?"

"Of course they will."

The girl wipes her eyes with her hands. "I am Auma, from the Otter Clan of the People of the Dawn-land, and this is Conkesema. She—"

My eyes go wide. "Conkesema! You're the Healer's daughter. Wakdanek's daughter."

Conkesema lets out a cry, then stutters uncontrollably as she scrambles across the ground on her knees to get to me. When she twines her hands in my cape and stares hard into my eyes, she gibbers. I don't understand any of her words, but I say, "Your father is here. Right now. He came with us to find you, to find both of you."

Conkesema lunges to her feet to run to find her father, and I grab her around the waist. Against her ear, I hiss, "Not yet. They'll kill you. We have to wait!"

She whines and sobs against my hair, *"No, no, no, no—"*

Auma gasps. "She's speaking! She hasn't spoken since the attack on our village."

I pull Conkesema down and say, "Wait. For now, that's all we can do."

The little girl sinks to the snow beside me, sitting so close I can barely move. Her gaze has fastened to my face and won't let go.

I notice that Wrass is subtly surveying the guards, who stand five paces away, and I wonder what he's looking at. The shorter man, whose name I don't know, has a bow and quiver slung over his left shoulder and carries a war club in his hand. He wears his hair in a long braid. Dakion has only a war club, though his belt bristles with stilettos, knives, and a throwing axe.

Dakion says, "I don't know how she knew...witchery...she said there would be a boy and a dog...all I did was... "

My heart flutters like a bird's after it's been shot with an arrow. I can't seem to catch my breath. She *knew* I would be there?

Dakion continues, "I'm relieving you. Go tell her where we're holding the two Yellowtail villagers...I'll wait...as she ordered, until... "

The shorter man says something low, then trots away into the darkness. Dakion props his war club on his shoulder.

Wrass tilts his head, motioning me to come closer. I slide away from Conkesema and go to sit by him. "Wrass, how could she have known that I would be there?"

"Doesn't matter now. Listen to me." He reaches into the knee-high moccasin on his wounded leg and pulls out a wooden stiletto. It is made from hardwood, probably maple, though I can't tell in the darkness, and has been ground to a sharp point. It's about three times as long as the deerbone stiletto that Sindak gave me. Long enough to puncture a lung or heart. Wrass hands it to me and says, "I made these in case I had to fight off wolves. I have another in my other moccasin, but I don't think I can... " He clenches his jaw to hold back tears. "When the time is right, you're going to have to do it, Odion."

Fear constricts my throat. I close my fingers around the smooth wood. It's warm from being close to his body. "All right, Wrass."

I'm scared, but not scared enough to fail him. Wrass risked his life to help me escape, and dying is less frightening to me than letting him down. I glance around at the other children and tuck the stiletto into my moccasin.

16

Sindak gritted his teeth and glared at the people in the firelight.

Gonda had Hehaka's thin body clutched against his chest and was growling, "Stop fighting me!"

The boy let out a shrill cry and kicked his legs harder. "No, I have to go to them. They're my family!"

Gonda glanced at his war club, bow, and quiver where they lay in the snow near the small fire, as though wishing he could grab one. Gonda, as well as he and Towa, still had deerbone stilettos tucked into their leggings, but none of them dared to reach for stilettos until they had no other choice.

"Let me go!" Hehaka shrieked.

"What about your father, the chief?" Gonda yelled in the boy's ear.

Hehaka's shrieking dropped to a wail. "He doesn't even remember me. He won't know who I am."

"No man ever forgets his son. He's probably spent most of his life trying to find you."

"No one came for me. No one! I used to lie awake praying someone would come. But no—"

"Hush!" Gonda ordered, and turned to watch Koracoo lithely stride into the firelight.

Her short hair clung wetly to her face, highlighting her slitted eyes. Out in the forest, whispers started as men began discussing her. They probably all knew her reputation...and that of Corpse-Eye. Sindak looked at the club resting in the snow. He was surprised no one had come to get it yet. Did that mean Gannajero needed every man exactly where he was?

Koracoo stopped two paces from Gonda, facing Kotin, and the man's gaze traced the line of her breasts, narrow waist, and lingered on her hips. He chuckled softly, as though she were already his.

Koracoo, who had undoubtedly endured such arrogance many times, called, "You're an outcast, little better than a slave. Where is your master?"

Kotin threw out his chest. "I speak for the mighty Gannajero."

"If Gannajero is here, why am I talking to you? Is she too cowardly to face me?"

Kotin chuckled again, and his yellow teeth

reflected the firelight like those of an old dog. "In a few moments, you'll all be dead. Why should she waste her time—?"

"Because,' Towa called, "I bring a message for her from the great Chief Atotarho."

Sindak spun to stare at his friend. As Towa marched past, Sindak said, "What are you doing?"

"Carrying out my chief's orders."

"What? *Now?*"

Towa gave him an irritated look, held up his hands, and continued into the firelight. The amber gleam turned Towa's buckskin cape golden and shaded every determined line in his handsome face.

"Kotin?" a warrior called from behind Towa.

"Let him come!" Kotin said with an exasperated look.

Towa walked to stand on the other side of Gonda so that the three of them—he, Towa, and Koracoo—formed a defensive line in front of the canoes.

"What's the message?" Kotin demanded to know.

When Towa shook his head, his long black hair swayed across the back of his cape. "My orders are to tell only Gannajero. Where is she?"

Kotin turned to his right, as though looking at someone who stood deep in the forest shadows.

Sindak followed his gaze, but saw nothing.

Then the brush rustled, parted, and an ugly old woman tramped out of the trees. Greasy twists of hair fell around her wrinkled face. Her lips were sucked in over toothless gums, but her eyes were like boiling cauldrons of sheer hatred.

"Gannajero! Gannajero!" Hehaka screamed, and threw himself into a fit in Gonda's arms.

Holding onto him must have been like clutching a wiry weasel with sharp claws. The boy scratched Gonda's face and throat until Gonda squeezed the air out of the boy's lungs and left him bug-eyed and gasping. "Don't fight me!"

Hehaka weakly pounded Gonda's shoulders. "I —I'll stop."

Gonda relaxed his hold enough to let the boy get a full breath of air into his lungs, whereupon Hehaka started sobbing.

The old woman didn't even glance at Hehaka as she walked over to Kotin. The shells and twists of copper on her cape shook with every move, creating small flashes in the near darkness.

"So," Gannajero said in a rough gravelly voice, "my brother sent a second messenger to follow the first. Smart. Do you carry the proof?"

Sindak wondered what she was talking about. Atotarho had already sent a messenger to her? Who? What message?

Towa cautiously walked toward her. "Is this what you're looking for?"

He grasped the leather thong around his neck and pulled the magnificent gorget over his head. When he held it out to her, the enormous carved shell swung back and forth. Kotin's jaw slackened in awe, probably calculating the extraordinary value, but Gannajero stood absolutely silent and still. Her gaze clung to the gorget, transfixed.

"Bring it here," she ordered, and extended a clawlike hand.

Towa shook his head. "Not until our negotiations are concluded. Atotarho wishes to make a Trade. He will—"

"Look around you, boy!" Gannajero said. "All I have to do is kill you and your friends and the gorget is mine!"

"Yes, but you won't have everything that goes with it. In exchange for the rights and privileges of owning this gorget, Atotarho wants both of his children back...and your guarantee that our party will not be harmed."

"He sold me and my brother into slavery when we'd seen eight summers, and he thinks I *owe* him something?"

The ground beneath Sindak's feet seemed to tremble. *That's* what had happened to the twins? Atotarho had sold the children into slavery? Blessed Spirits, it couldn't be true.

"He doesn't think you owe him anything. He thinks you *want* something. In exchange, he demands his children." The gorget dangling from Towa's hand lowered a little. "That is the Trade."

Gannajero vented a low disbelieving laugh. "When he sent me his four-summers-old son, his only condition was that I keep the boy alive, and keep my mouth shut. In exchange, once a summer, he sent me a messenger with big bags of pearls. Do you understand? He willingly let me have Hehaka. All these summers, I made Hehaka go through every horror I did as a child. Now, suddenly, my brother offers me everything I've ever dreamed of? Why?"

Koracoo flexed her fists. "Do you agree to the Trade, or not?"

Gannajero shook her head, as though denying some inner admonition. "It's not enough."

Towa shifted. "What do you mean 'not enough'? He's offering you the rulership—"

"I know what he's offering, imbecile. My brother, the *great* Chief Atotarho, grew rich and powerful off spoils that should have been mine!" She thumped her chest. "I'm the one who should have been living in comfort, wielding the power of the clan. But for thirty summers—"

"He only wants his children."

"You already have Hehaka." She waved a hand in the boy's direction and turned slightly away, checking the positions of her warriors.

"M-me?" Hehaka said in a tiny pained voice.

He pushed back to stare at Gonda. "The chief wants me?"

"Of course he does," Gonda said.

Hehaka threw himself into a kicking frenzy. "No! I'm staying with Gannajero and Kotin. They're my family!"

As though the hidden meaning of the transaction had just dawned on Koracoo, she leveled a glare at Towa. "Hold on. What do you mean 'rulership'? What are these rights and privileges Chief Atotarho is promising?"

Towa swallowed hard. "The chief, and his clan, are offering to restore Gannajero to her rightful position as matron of the Wolf Clan. If she accepts, she will become the most powerful woman in our world."

Koracoo's eyes narrowed, and Sindak knew exactly what she must be feeling: insensible rage. After all the things the old woman had done to their children, and scores of others, her clan was going to reward her?

Gonda lowered Hehaka to the ground and softly said, "Get in the canoe."

Hehaka turned to look pleadingly at Gannajero. The old woman shooed him toward the boat. "Do as he says. Get in the canoe."

"But...don't you want me? I want to go with you!"

"Want you? I never wanted you. You were my revenge. Get in the canoe!"

Tears filled Hehaka's eyes. He waited for a few more moments, as though certain she would change her mind. When it was obvious she wasn't going to, he ran for the canoe. Whimpering, he climbed past Baji and Tutelo, then over the packs to go sit in the rear, as far away from the commotion as he could get. Wakdanek said something to him, and Hehaka jerked a nod, but Sindak couldn't hear their exchange.

"What about Zateri?" Towa asked.

Gannajero extended her hand again. "Let me see the gorget first. I want to know it's genuine."

Towa hesitated. After several moments, he apparently convinced himself it would do her no good to possess it without the rest of the bargain being fulfilled, so he walked forward and extended the thong. Her fingers clamped around it like a bear's jaws, and she lifted the carved shell to examine it in the firelight. Her lips moved, as though speaking to it, or perhaps counting something. Her eyes widened.

"It's true," she said in a stunned voice. "It's real." After five more heartbeats, her cold gaze lifted. "What's the trap?"

Towa stared at her. "There's no trap. He wants his children."

She chuckled darkly. "That hardly seems like him."

Kotin moved closer to her to stare at it and said, "What about the rest? When do you get all the riches?"

"When I return to the village, fool! Did you think my brother would send a flotilla of canoes carrying all the wealth of the Wolf Clan? Of course not. We—"

"Our business is not finished," Towa interrupted. Gannajero turned to glare at him, and he repeated, "Where is Zateri?"

Gannajero slowly, reverently, slipped the thong around her neck and adjusted the gorget. It covered her entire chest. "What are your orders once we've concluded our negotiations?"

Sindak had been wondering the same thing. It bewildered him that after all they'd been through, Towa had remained loyal to Atotarho.

Towa's expression was grim when he said, "My orders are to obey you as the new high matron of Atotarho Village and to protect you until you arrive home."

Sindak blurted, "What? You're joking! She's a monster!" Sindak felt betrayed. The Wolf Clan intended to bring this evil old woman back to live among the children of the other clans? *Horrific.* No one would stand for it.

"Those are our orders, Sindak," Towa replied through a taut exhalation.

Gannajero's jet-black eyes darted from face to face. "And are your cohorts also obliged to serve me?" Her gaze fixed on Koracoo.

A humorless smile turned Koracoo's lips. "Of course," she replied, much to Towa's surprise. "Once the Trade is made, our duty is to help escort you and the children back to Atotarho Village."

"We will follow you in our own canoe, War Chief," Gannajero said suspiciously. "So we can keep track of your treachery."

Kotin said, "When do we get paid? We don't have to follow you all the way back to Atotarho Village, do we?"

As she stroked the gorget, Gannajero offhandedly replied, "Open my small pack. Pay the new men we hired yesterday. Separate the contents of the pack into six equal piles. Once we are finished here, they're free to go."

Kotin walked into the trees and grabbed her pack. As he walked back, he called, "You men. Come down."

Five warriors trotted into the firelight; then another swerved around Sindak and loped forward. As Kotin doled out strings of pearls, shell gorgets, bags of beads, and sheets of pounded copper, the men giggled and danced around like children.

Gannajero said, "Pick up your earnings and

return to your positions. You are still mine until this is finished."

The warriors grabbed their earnings and ran back to their positions, smiling and yipping like demented dogs.

Gannajero turned to her own men. "The rest of you have a choice to make. You can either split my four packs, or you can pledge yourselves to the new matron of the Wolf Clan, and earn vastly more as my personal guards. If you decide to—"

Towa shouted, "*Zateri*. Where is Zateri?"

Gannajero paused, grunted, then lifted a hand and motioned to one of the men in the trees. "Waswan, bring the girl."

A very thin man with a broken nose came out of the darkness shoving a girl before him. Zateri was even smaller and more slender than Sindak recalled. She was wearing a blue-painted cape that was much too big for her. It dragged the ground. At some point in the past moon, she'd cut her hair short in mourning. It hung around her chin in irregular black locks.

Koracoo ordered, "Put her in the canoe with the other children."

Waswan's inhuman eyes went to Gannajero, and the old woman nodded. "Do as she says."

As Waswan marched Zateri to the canoe, he laughed and taunted, "I'm going to miss you, Chipmunk Teeth," and he groped her young breasts.

Koracoo's eyes flashed with rage, and Sindak's breathing went swift and shallow. Before they reached home, he was going to kill that man.

Zateri climbed into the canoe, and Tutelo and Baji leaped forward to hug her in a tearful reunion. He heard Zateri say, "Where's Odion?"

"Now," Koracoo said with a threatening tilt of her head. "Where are the other children?"

"You mean the two Yellowtail Village children?" Kotin said. "They're safe."

"Not just the Yellowtail children," Koracoo responded. "We want all the children, no matter their nation."

"We didn't promise you *all* the children," Kotin insisted. "Only your own—"

"Let them have them." Gannajero turned to one of the Dawnland men and barked, "You. Go fetch Dakion and the other brats. Bring them here."

"Yes, Gannajero."

After he'd trotted away into the darkness, Gannajero scowled at her remaining men. Kotin was seething. He looked like he longed to get his hands around her throat. Gannajero said, "Well? Which of you is willing to serve as the personal guard to the matron of the Wolf Clan of the Hills People?"

Waswan trotted up and grinned. Kotin continued standing beside her, but he made no sign of assent.

From behind Sindak, a man shouted, "I'll take what's in your packs."

Kotin growled, "You've always been worthless, Ojib! You disloyal cur!"

"Give him half the packs," Gannajero said.

"Half!" Kotin objected. His mouth hung open. "You were going to force four of us to split four packs—that's one each. Now you're giving Ojib *two*."

"Do as I say! You're going to get far more over the next few summers."

"But I was supposed to get the two Dawnland girls that you just gave away! If Ojib gets two packs, I want the other two as compensation!"

"You can't have them. When Dakion returns, he may want to be paid, and what will I—?"

Sindak flinched when he heard the hiss of an arrow behind him and, from the corner of his eye, saw Ojib fall. The arrow had taken him through the throat. He was trying to scream, but couldn't. Five heartbeats later, Cord appeared, slit the man's throat to silence him forever, and then lifted a hand to get Sindak's attention. When he knew Sindak was looking at him, he pointed to his own chest, and Sindak nodded, understanding that he was to wait for Cord's signal. Cord slipped back into the darkness.

A flush of hope filtered hotly through Sindak.

There was no one behind him now. As Kotin

and Gannajero's argument grew louder, all attention fastened upon them.

Kotin shouted, "This isn't the first time you've promised me girls and then sold them out from under me. Two moons ago—"

"Stop whining! I've already told you I'll pay you for your losses when we get to—"

Sindak reached down, picked up his club, and tucked it beneath his cape. Next, he sidled forward to stand beside CorpseEye. Slowly, he lowered his hand and grasped the legendary club. As he rose again, he hid it behind his back, and it was as though Koracoo felt his hands upon the weapon. A shiver went through her. She turned to look at Sindak...and smiled.

17

A few of the Dawnland men kept glancing uneasily back into the trees, as though they sensed Cord's presence, but the fire had obviously blinded them. They squinted, fidgeted with their bows, and turned back to watch Gannajero and Kotin. The old woman was shouting in his face.

Cord dropped to his knees atop a low hill with a clear view of the camp and pulled six arrows from his quiver, laying them out in a neat row at his side. By now, he trusted Sindak had collected weapons.

Cord nocked his bow and sucked in a deep steadying breath. As he sighted down the shaft, he heard steps just barely crunch the snow behind him.

I'm dead.

He clenched his jaw, waiting for the impact of the arrow.

When it didn't come, he shot a glance over his shoulder. Black Cape stood three paces away with his gaze focused on Gannajero. There was a bizarre quality to the man, a stillness so total it was as though he had been standing behind Cord for thousands of summers, waiting for this moment. He had his pale hands folded in front of him, and Cord noticed for the first time that he wore sandals, as though he was immune to the cold.

In an unsettlingly soft voice, Black Cape said, "She was telling the truth, you know. Our brother did sell us into slavery when we'd seen eight summers." Heavy lids gave his eyes a sleepy expression that made their unnatural wolfish gleam even more sinister.

"You're her brother?"

"Her twin."

Cord saw no resemblance, except that they both had utterly mad eyes.

"Shortly after that, we were sold again, to different men in distant villages. I didn't see her for another ten summers. She had just bought her first children." Hatred inflected the tones, but subtly. "I was a warrior. I had been with the war party that attacked the village. She came to our camp to purchase some of the orphans we'd rounded up as slaves." He hesitated, as though he had all the time on earth to finish this story. "At first I-I wasn't sure it was her. Then I saw the gorget she'd made for herself. It was as though she believed she was matron of the Wolf Clan, as though nothing had ever happened to us. I couldn't stand it. I stole the gorget and freed every child. Most of them made it home. Alive or dead. I made sure. I carried them in my arms."

Cord slightly eased off his drawn bow. "I want to hear the rest, believe me I do, but right now—"

"Don't kill her. The others, yes, but not her." He spoke as though he weren't breathing; his chest did not move with air.

Somehow, it reminded Cord to exhale the lungful of air he'd unwittingly been holding. "Why not? She is the problem, my friend. Her men are just—"

"Yes," he answered in a sad voice. "She has always been the 'problem.' But there are many who have claims on her life. You are not one of them."

Cord shook his head. The obsidian eyes held his. The man did not blink or look away. No expression lined his face, only a strange serenity far more frightening than anger.

"And if I do kill her?" Cord asked.

Black Cape moved his pale hands, reclasping them. It was a sort of weightless gesture, as quiet as the light snowfall, and Cord had the distinct impression that he was not flesh and blood. The man said, "You must help me with this one thing. It is not your right to kill her." The desperation in his voice never touched the glassy stillness of his face. He remained oddly immobile, as if centuries had taught him that, like the serpent in the leaves, survival rested in stillness.

As the voices in the camp rose to a crescendo, Cord became acutely conscious of the blood surging in his veins. It was now or never. "Very well," he said, "but I can't speak for anyone else."

Black Cape's head moved faintly, a dip of gratitude that seemed stripped to bare bones, a far-off echo of a human gesture. The man's gaze shifted to Gannajero. There was an instant of terrible silence where Cord had the feeling he was gazing upon a starving monster biding its time, motionless, waiting to strike until the prey came close enough.

Cord drew back his bow, aimed, and released. Before the arrow had even struck Kotin, he had another arrow nocked and aimed at Waswan.

He let fly, and glanced at Black Cape. The creature seemed frozen in time.

Cord nocked his bow and drew back again, but a hail of arrows began striking the trees around him. Cord flattened himself behind the hill as shouts went up and men started running for cover.

"Get down!" Cord yelled.

Black Cape just stood serenely staring at Gannajero, as though oblivious to the rain of death.

18

Sindak's muscles hardened and swelled against his leather shirt as he waited for Cord. What was taking him so long? Sindak's hand ached where he was gripping CorpseEye, hiding the club behind his back. To make things more interesting, CorpseEye had started to warm his fingers, and it terrified him. Was the club trying to tell him something? What was he supposed to do about it?

Gannajero and Kotin's argument had grown violent. The old woman was shoving Kotin with both hands while he waved his war club. He must have been weighing the momentary pleasure of beating her to bloody pulp for humiliating him in front of his warriors against the next twenty summers of untold wealth, and perhaps even status as the matron's personal guard—

An arrow flashed in the firelight, the chert point glinting as it drove into Kotin's back with enough force to send him staggering drunkenly across the ground.

One of the warriors shouted, "We're being attacked! Kill them!"

"No!" Gannajero yelled. "If you kill them, I lose everything!"

Before anyone could react, another arrow *shish-thumped* into Waswan, and the man let out a hideous cry. Then a melee broke out. Shouts and screams rose. Men started running in all directions. Two men launched themselves at Gonda and knocked him to the ground, while several others wildly fired arrows into the darkness, trying to stop their attacker.

Sindak lunged into the clearing, shouting, "War Chief!" and when Koracoo turned, he tossed her CorpseEye.

As it spun through the air toward her, her eyes lit with a feral gleam. Koracoo snatched the weapon out of the air, pivoted on one foot, and charged into the fight spinning and leaping like some Spirit creature from the old stories. Two men sprang at her, grinning and whooping. She used a side-handed swing to crush the shoulder of the first and send him stumbling for the forest; then she spun on her toes and knocked the feet out from under the second man. Before he had time to roll, she brought her club down on his skull and moved on, running deeper into the fight.

A big warrior with missing front teeth shrieked a war cry and barreled toward Sindak, his club up. Sindak had just enough time to pull his own club from his belt and parry a blow meant to crush his skull, but the force of the assault toppled him. As he scrambled to get up, the warrior hissed, "Die, Hills dog!" and swung his club down hard, aimed for Sindak's spine.

Sindak rolled. The club whomped the ground less than a hand's breadth from his body. Gasping for breath, Sindak clawed his way to his feet, and they circled each other like buffalo bulls, growling and panting.

"Are all your men so slow?" Sindak taunted with a grin. "Or are your knees just weak from rutting with your sisters?"

"You filth!"

Their clubs collided with arm-numbing force, and the man's superior weight drove Sindak back five steps before he recovered, side-stepped, and slammed his club into the man's chest. As the man stumbled backward, gasping, Sindak took the opportunity to cave in his ribs.

Then he charged for the fracas around the fire. His gaze instinctively searched for Towa...but his friend had vanished. Gannajero was gone, too. Towa hadn't dragged her off to protect her, had he?

Despite their chief's orders, the old woman deserved to be dead a thousand times over. And Towa knew it just as well as he did.

"Sindak?" Wakdanek cried. He was fighting a losing battle against three warriors, trying to keep them from getting to the canoes and the children. They were taking turns swinging at him, forcing him backward while they laughed. Sindak's gaze briefly flitted to the canoe, noting that he didn't see Baji or Zateri. Were they hiding beneath the packs?

Sindak swerved for Wakdanek just as an arrow *zizzed* by his ear. *Blessed gods!* He gasped in surprise, thinking it was meant for him, but the arrow neatly sliced through the chest of one of Wakdanek's opponents. *Cord* was still alive! The enemy staggered, looked down at the brightly fletched shaft protruding from his lungs, and a bizarre smile lit his face before he collapsed to his knees and started howling.

With only two left, Sindak shouted, "Wakdanek? Take the canoe. Get the children out of here!" and leaped a war club aimed at his knees. Before the man could recover, Sindak crushed his right hip and was spinning for the last man. "Go on!"

The big Healer leaped forward, shoved the canoe away from the shore, and ducked a whistling arrow as he madly paddled out into the current. The other canoe sat alone on the bank.

The last man roared and charged Sindak. Sindak skipped sideways. The momentum of the man's rush carried him past. Before Sindak could batter his brains out, an arrow slashed through Sindak's left shoulder and punched through the other side just above his collarbone, pinning his cape to his chest and rendering his left arm useless.

"Ha!" his opponent crowed. "You're a dead man."

Panic seized Sindak, but he managed to lift his club to block the warrior's next blow.

As the man lifted his club again, he bellowed, "Now, Hills coward, die!"

Sindak jerked when an arrow pierced the back of the man's skull. The warrior staggered, and his mouth opened as though to scream, but he just fell to the ground and started shuddering spastically.

Cradling his wounded arm, Sindak ran for cover. He got into the trees through a shower of arrows and dropped to his knees behind a head-high pile of deadfall. In the snow, he saw the small tracks of two children. They'd been running.

"Think about it later," he whispered to himself as he propped his club against a fallen log and gripped the blood-slick arrow that pierced his shoulder. He gritted his teeth to prepare himself, snapped the tip off, then reached behind him for the fletched shaft. When he jerked it out of his back, it was as though the cry was ripped from his throat by a jagged fishhook. The pain left him panting breathlessly.

From the edge of his vision, he saw several of the enemy warriors fleeing into the forest.

Fighting nausea, he forced himself to pick up his club again. He saw Gonda get stabbed in the side, but the wound didn't slow the man down. Gonda jerked the deerbone stiletto from his legging and plunged it into the throat of the man on top of him; then he rolled and scrambled to his feet just as another warrior swung his club at Gonda's head. Gonda ducked and drove himself headfirst into the man's stomach, bowling him backward, where they both collapsed to the ground. As they grunted and gasped, struggling for the club, Sindak searched the clearing. Dead men scattered the ground. CorpseEye had cut a swath through the enemy. No one was left standing.

Where is Koracoo?

Was she down? He didn't see her. Had she followed someone into the forest? Baji and Zateri?

No...there were no adult tracks mixed with those of the children.

Terror chittered through Sindak's souls. Koracoo wanted Gannajero dead...and Towa was sworn to protect her. Had she gone after Towa?

Gonda let out a hoarse cry, pulled the club from his opponent's grasp, and brought it down squarely in the middle of the man's skull. The sodden crack echoed through the trees. As though completely spent, Gonda collapsed on top of the dead man. He just lay there for several moments, breathing, before he rolled off and began probing the stab wound in his side.

Soft whimpers erupted behind Sindak, and he turned to see Gitchi staggering up the trail. Blood covered the wolf puppy's head, and one of his eyes had swollen closed. He kept stumbling, wobbling, obviously clubbed. The wolf braced his shaking legs and lifted his nose to sniff the breeze, looking eastward; then he let out a low growl.

Through the wavering firelit shadows, Sindak made out two men. One crouched on the hilltop twenty paces away. The other stood beside him, clearly visible, seemingly unaware that he made a perfect target.

Moments later, Cord rose and trotted out of the trees. He carried his nocked bow and scanned the clearing as he ran for Sindak. The other man remained standing alone in the darkness.

Cord said, "Where's Gannajero?"

"I don't know. I was occupied when she left. Who were you talking to up there?" He tipped his chin toward the man.

"A friend. I think. I'll explain when we have less pressing concerns. Wakdanek made it away?"

"Yes. But I didn't see Zateri or Baji in the canoe, and I don't know where Towa went. He may have thought it was his duty to carry out our chief's orders and protect that miserable old woman. If so—"

"Koracoo went after him?" The serpent tattooed on Cord's cheeks writhed as he grimaced.

"I think so. I have to find Towa before she does. I have to talk to him."

He gestured to Sindak's shoulder. It was streaming blood down his cape. "Are you able?"

"I'll manage."

"Then go. I'll care for Gonda's wounds."

19
ODION

Dakion hisses, "Shut your mouths! I can't hear anything," and cocks his ear to the night.

I hold my breath and listen. The other children go still. Someone is coming. We all hear feet rapidly slogging through the snow; then we hear cursing. As the man climbs the low hill just beyond the clearing, a thin layer of Cloud People cover Grandmother Moon, and her light dims. The distant chaos of screams and shouts carries on the freezing wind. We've heard it off and on for about one finger of time. The longer it takes Mother and Father to come striding over that rise, the more my stomach aches. I fight not to imagine what happens if they are both killed and Gannajero is the one who returns.

"Dakion?" a man calls from below the rise, and Dakion rushes to look down the slope.

"What? What's happening? I keep hearing the sounds of—"

"So do I!" The man appears on the crest of the hill. He is of medium height, with an oval face and a pug nose. He stands before Dakion, breathing hard. "When I left, everything was under control. I have to get back immediately. You have to bring the children. Follow my tracks and you'll have no trouble finding the camp on the river."

"Bring the children! Are you insane? What good—?"

"That's what the old woman wants. In exchange for the children, Chief Atotarho and the Wolf Clan have offered her the leadership of Atotarho Village. Whoever chooses to serve as one of her personal guards will be rich beyond his wildest imaginings. Now, bring the children!" The man turns and runs back, slipping and sliding, disappearing over the hill.

Dakion licks his lips and grumbles something under his breath, as though deciding whether or not he will follow Gannajero's orders.

Wrass looks at me, and I shake my head. I can't believe that Chief Atotarho would...

Wrass whispers, "Two days ago, a man found Gannajero alone at our camp and told her that in exchange for 'both of them' her brother would fulfill her dreams. Do you think Atotarho—?"

"Is her brother? I know he is."

Dakion snarls, "Shut up, brats! Get on your feet. We're going to the river."

Auma and Conkesema rise. I try to help Wrass up, but he cries out the instant I lift him. "I can't do it, Dakion! Leave me. I'll be here when you get back."

Dakion stalks over the hill with a hateful gleam in his eyes. "I'm not coming back. No one is. You're not worth the effort."

As he strides for Wrass, Auma and Conkesema back away, and I lock my knees. The wooden stiletto in my moccasin seems to be growing larger, pressing against my leg.

Conkesema whimpers when Dakion lifts his war club over Wrass's head and says, "I've wanted to do this for a long time."

Wrass throws up his arms to block the blow and cries, *"No!"* just as I grab the stiletto, step into the space below Dakion's uplifted arms, and plunge the weapon repeatedly into his chest, belly, arms— anything I can reach. Someone is shrieking, but it takes me a long time to realize it's my own voice. From the corner of my eye, I see the war club swinging toward me, but it seems to take forever to impact my shoulder and drive me into the ground. I hear bone snap and topple to the snow.

For a few instants, the world goes black; when my eyes see again, Wrass is on top of Dakion, plunging his stiletto into the man's chest over and over. Every time he pulls the stiletto loose, the wooden tip slings blood, but Wrass can't stop. Dakion is still weakly flailing and trying to yell, though the only thing that bubbles from his throat is blood. Wrass does not stop until Dakion goes limp and his eyes fixedly stare at the snowflakes drifting out of the gleaming sky. Even then, Wrass hesitates with the stiletto poised over Dakion's already mutilated heart, waiting for him to rise again. When it's clear that he's dead, Wrass sobs and crawls away, dragging his injured foot behind him. The first thing he says is, "Odion? Are you all right?"

I shake my head. The pain is stunning. I'm crying breathlessly. "I-I think he broke by shoulder. My collarbone. I—"

"Odion, listen to me. You have to go look for the other man. Did he hear us and turn around?"

Fear surges through me. I drag myself to my feet, whimpering in pain, and trot over the crest of the hill. The forest below is still and glistening. "No, he's gone. I think we're safe." I tuck the bloody stiletto into my belt and pull my left arm against my chest. Without warning, I throw up. The agony runs through my entire body. I gasp, "We should run."

Wrass is sobbing brokenly, but he nods. "I can't, Odion. But the three of you have to. You-you're the leader now. Make sure they're safe."

A strange feeling comes over me. Wrass has passed the mantle of leadership to me, but I'm terrified and hurt. "Wrass, I don't...think I can. I—"

"Yes, you can," he insists. "Now get away from

here! When Dakion doesn't show up in the camp, they'll send more warriors. You can't be here when they arrive!"

I vomit again. When I finally turn to Auma and Conkesema, I'm choking on my own bile, but I manage to say, "Follow me. We're going to run east, away from the river."

Auma squares her young shoulders and calmly says, "All right. But first, let's take Dakion's weapons. We're going to need them."

Her sensibilities in the face of extreme danger leave me in awe. "You're right. Take them all. We'll divide them later."

The three of us trot back to his body and begin stripping it of weapons. Auma takes the axe and two deerbone stilettos, while Conkesema gingerly pulls a hafted knife from Dakion's belt. My head is spinning when I pick up the man's war club, then his bow and quiver. I carry the bow down to Wrass and lay it, along with the quiver, beside him. "The moonlight is bright. Don't let them get too close."

Wrass smiles gratefully and pulls the bow and quiver onto his lap. As he nocks an arrow, he stammers, "Not if I can help it."

The pain in my shoulder has grown so stunning I can't stop the tears that flow down my cheeks, but I call, "Auma? Conkesema? Let's go."

The girls fall into line behind me, and I start

leading them out into the gloom, trudging through the light snow.

I'm praying that Mother and Father have already killed Gannajero's party and are, even now, trying to find me. But the past moon has taught me that I can't count on anyone rescuing me or my friends. We have to save ourselves. As my breathing begins to return to normal, the horrifying realization is sinking in. I killed a man. I can't feel my left hand, but the blood on my right has grown sticky. It glues my fingers to the war club. The only thing that helps keep my souls from fleeing my body is the fact that if I hadn't killed Dakion, Wrass would now be dead, killed with this very club, and I might be dead as well.

We haven't gone more than one hundred paces when I hear something. Ahead of us, on the other side of a wall of brush, *someone* is walking toward us...

"Shh!" I hiss, and extend the war club to block Auma and Conkesema from taking another step.

The feet are almost silent. Warriors fleeing the fight? I take a new grip on the club. The pain in my shoulder is unbearable, but I have to concentrate and do what I must to give Auma and Conkesema a chance to run. *Stay focused. Focus!*

Two dark shapes appear and disappear through the brush. Just before they emerge, one stops and whispers something to his companion. Then both charge from the brush at dead runs, heading straight for me.

Zateri shouts, *"Odion? Odion!"*

Hot blood stings my veins. I can't help it. The mixture of hope and relief is so great, I stagger and can barely stay on my feet. My knees long to buckle. "Zateri? Baji?"

Zateri rushes to hug me, but hesitates when she sees my bloody shoulder. She stops and just stands in front of me, tears in her eyes. She is a head shorter than I am, and the arm she extends to tenderly touch my good shoulder is skinny. "We were so afraid we'd be too late. As soon as we could escape, we came looking for you."

Baji breaks in. "Where's Wrass? Is he...?" Baji's eyes suddenly go huge. She is looking to my right, toward the brush.

I jerk around and see a hunched form weaving through the tangle of branches. *No...it can't be...my heart won't let me believe...*

Baji turns to Auma. "I don't know who you are, girl, but give me that axe you're carrying."

Baji's tone is commanding. Auma instantly hands it over.

"And I want one of those stilettos," Zateri says, and extends a hand to Auma, who pulls it from her belt and places it in Zateri's hand.

Auma sobs, "What if it's a warrior? What are we going to do? We can't fight! We have to run!" She starts to back away.

"You can run if you want to," I whisper. "But I can't. I won't. Not ever again." Though I can barely walk, I stiffen my spine and stagger toward the brush.

"I'm right behind you, Odion," Baji says.

"So am I." Zateri's steps are catlike.

20

As the Cloud People drifted through the night sky, the landscape alternated from pitch black to moon-silvered in a matter of moments. When moonlight streamed through the maples, Koracoo picked out the trail again. Dredged through ankle-deep snow, it cast a crooked black line through the white. Towa was taking the old woman away from the river and out into the dark depths of the forest where gigantic trees loomed.

Koracoo silently paralleled his course. After spending almost one moon on the trail together, she knew Towa: He had an implacable sense of honor. Following his chief's orders must be tearing him apart. But would he kill her to save Gannajero?

Ahead, a tangled stack of rotted timbers created a dark wall. The trail vanished when the clouds shifted, melting into the utter blackness. Five heartbeats later, it reappeared silvered in moonlight, veered wide around the deadfall, and snaked back into a grove of maples. A few old leaves clung to the branches and rattled in the breeze, but Koracoo heard no human sounds. No feet crunching snow. No whispers.

She circled the deadfall, keeping her eyes on the fallen timbers. The tangle made a perfect hiding place. Wind Mother whistled through the dead branches, carrying the earthy fragrance of decaying wood. One step at a time, she followed the wide curve past the deadfall and halted behind a massive sycamore trunk.

Cloud People darkened the sky again, briefly turning the world dark and cold. She shivered beneath her cape. Her shirt was sweat-soaked from the fight. Now that her body was cooling, the warmth was draining out of her muscles. When the clouds moved on, snowflakes pirouetted from the heavens like white wisps of eagle down, softly alighting on the ground and branches around her.

Koracoo gripped CorpseEye in both hands and examined the way the trail slithered around the tree trunks, heading off to—

A carefully placed foot squealed in the snow behind her. She knew how he moved.

Without turning, she called, "Towa? Let's talk."

"Toss CorpseEye aside and spread your arms, then turn around."

Koracoo reluctantly did as he'd instructed and turned to face him. In the icy wind, his long black hair played around his broad shoulders. She said, "Do you have any idea what you're doing? This is wrong, Towa."

As he walked closer to her, his cape swayed around his long legs. "I know you want to kill her. So do I. The gods know she deserves to die for what she's done, but I can't let that happen."

"Do you trust Atotarho? Really? You actually believe the Wolf Clan is going to install her as the new clan matron?"

As Towa came nearer, she could see his grimace. He was having a very hard time with this. "If they do, it's a death sentence. It may be her birthright, but the other clans will instantly start plotting her murder."

"Then I doubt that she'll live more than a few days after you get her home."

"I doubt it, too. But it's still my duty to get her there."

"I admire your loyalty to your chief, Towa, but why would he give you such orders when he knows the other clans will never allow her to rule? You need to think this through, before you—"

"I have." Towa nervously licked his lips. "I've done little else over the past moon. My guess is that once he gets her home, he's going to turn her into some sort of prize he can parade around to elevate his status among our people. He'll boast that he captured her; then he'll send word out to all the surrounding villages so he can sacrifice her to the cheers of a huge crowd."

"Blessed Spirits." Koracoo's hard jaw went slack. Towa had always been the thinker, the one who worked a problem every step of the way until his conclusion was more than probable; it was a near certainty. "That makes perfect sense."

"The irony is that the only way he could get her to go along with it was to send her the most cherished artifact of his clan—the Horned Serpent gorget. She'd have never believed him otherwise. Never once in the entire history of our people has the gorget left the hands of our leader. Sending it to her was a stroke of genius."

A flush of revelation sent heat surging through Koracoo. "This journey had nothing to do with rescuing his children, did it?"

Towa gestured weakly. "The only thing I can say for certain is that the story convinced you to help him. You'd have never helped him if it hadn't been for Zateri, would you?"

She laughed softly. "No." It didn't matter now. She had more important things to worry about. "Did Gannajero tell you where she'd hidden Odion and the other children?"

148 W. MICHAEL GEAR & KATHLEEN O'NEAL GEAR

"Somewhere in the forest, that's all I know, but they can't be far away."

Koracoo closed her extended hands to fists. "What are your plans, Towa? You going to kill me to keep me from killing her...even knowing she's destined to die shortly after you get her home?"

He braced his legs. In an agonized voice, he replied, "From the first instant that Chief Atotarho pulled me into his longhouse and gave me these orders, I've been sick to my stomach. I hate this, Koracoo. But please don't force me to make that choice. I can't—"

"No, you can't, good friend," Sindak called from the darkness. "I won't let you do something you'll regret for the rest of your very short life."

Towa spun to look at Sindak. Though Koracoo couldn't see him, apparently Towa could. He stared directly into the darkness near the tangled wall of deadfall and said, "What do you mean 'very short life'?"

"I mean, if you make any move to kill Koracoo, I'll have to kill you. And doing so will destroy my life, Towa. I love you like a brother."

"Sindak, what am I supposed to do? Disobey the orders of our chief? How can I ever go home and face my family—?"

"Atotarho isn't worthy of your loyalty. Don't you know that by now? All of this has been an exquisitely well-planned ruse to elevate his status.

It wouldn't surprise me if Akio was an unwitting part of it, just like we were."

Towa's head cocked. "Are you saying he wasn't a traitor?"

"Of course he wasn't. Zateri was the bait to draw Gannajero in. If the chief had called Akio into his longhouse and given him special secret orders to make sure his daughter was captured, Akio would have been just as goggle-eyed with loyalty as you are tonight."

"You mean...that's why the chief went out on that Trading mission? It was the setup to make sure his daughter was captured?"

"Makes sense, doesn't it? You always wondered why he picked the two worst warriors in the village—you and me—to undertake the mission of rescuing his beloved daughter. The only thing that makes it worse is that he actually picked the *three* worst warriors: you, me, and Akio. He must have thought we were idiots. Of course we've proven that, haven't we? Especially you."

As Towa's aim began to quake and dip toward the ground, Koracoo said, "Towa, we need to know where Odion and the other children are. Where did you stash the old woman? We have to ask her."

Sindak called, "Stop being an idiot. Tell her, Towa."

Towa let out a shaky breath and closed his eyes.

He gestured to the right with his bow. "She's over there, hidden in that copse of dogwoods."

Koracoo's eyes narrowed. The copse was only twenty paces away, close enough that the old woman could have heard every word they'd—

Koracoo grabbed CorpseEye and lunged for the dogwoods, running with the club out in front of her to help her keep her balance in the slick snow. When she veered around the dogwoods, she saw the place the old woman had stood, listening and watching. The snow had been tamped down from constantly shifting feet.

Koracoo shouted, "She's gone!"

21

As Gannajero waded through the snow, headed south to where they'd stowed their canoes on the riverbank, she burned with rage. Most, maybe all, of her men were dead. She could always hire more—that wasn't the problem. In the past twenty summers, she'd hidden stashes of wealth in ten different places—enough to pay an army if necessary. One of her stashes was less than two days north of here. In four or five days, she'd be back to Trading as vigorously as before. But she had to make it to a canoe before dawn. Her trail through the ankle-deep snow was impossible to hide. The instant War Chief Koracoo had enough light to track, she would come, hunting like a starving wolf following a hapless rabbit.

Gannajero grasped the upthrust branch of a

fallen maple and studied the moonlit forest. The gleaming silver patina that covered the trees seemed dull in contrast to the brilliant snow. Ahead, a small clearing created an irregular oval on the low hillside. A deer trail threaded across the snow and through a thicket of brush, then wound through the middle of the clearing. She stepped onto the deer trail and plodded forward. If she were lucky, several deer would run this trail throughout the night, obliterating her tracks. But that would only slow Koracoo down.

As Gannajero headed for the clearing, her rage grew to a conflagration. Her brother thought he could trap her by sending her the sacred gorget! *And it had almost worked.* All of her life, she had dreamed of that gorget. Her earliest memory was of her mother slipping it over her head and saying, "Someday this will be yours." Though Gannajero wasn't allowed to play with it, she used to sit next to her mother in council and stare at it. She had counted the stars and knew every graceful curve and color variation in the carving. Deep inside her, in the dark space between her souls, the gorget's voice lived. It had called to her for thirty-two summers. Even when she was far away in distant alien empires, it begged her to come home. That's why twenty-five summers ago, she'd made an exact copy for herself. Carved it from memory with painstaking attention to detail. Though she'd known it wasn't the sacred artifact, it had comforted her. At least until her demented brother stole it from her.

Her gnarled hand rose to caress the gorget where it lay upon her chest. So many times she had tried to get home. Once, when she'd seen sixteen summers, she'd made it to the gates of her village— by then it was called Atotarho Village—only to be told by her brother's henchmen that she was an impostor. The Wolf Clan said that Atotarho's only sister was long dead. They'd dispatched a war party to drive her away.

"My brother, the great Atotarho, couldn't stand to look into my eyes."

She followed the trail through the brush, and when she emerged, movement on the far side of the clearing caught her eye. It resembled a black spider stepping across the snow on three enormous long legs. Occasionally beads or shells flashed in the moonlight. Then she realized with a start that the "legs" were actually long shadows being cast by three—

A single high-pitched cry of recognition pierced the trees. She gasped and ran. Feet thrashed the snow behind her. Wailing at the tops of their lungs, their voices blended to create one inhuman cry. She kept stumbling over roots and rocks hidden beneath the snow, falling and dragging herself to her feet, plunging on.

Her legging caught on a piece of deadfall and flung her forward. Before she could thrust out her arms to cushion the fall, she hit the ground hard, and the platter-sized gorget made a loud crack.

"No!"

When she sat up, she saw half the gorget shining in the snow. Her hand shot out to retrieve it...and they closed in around her.

Their pale faces seemed to have no other features than eyes. Huge black eyes. Their chests were rising and falling swiftly.

They were just children. Little more than scared mice. Gannajero rolled to her knees and shouted, "Get away from me before I witch you and rip your hearts from your bodies, you stupid brats!"

That high-pitched scream erupted again. It was earsplitting. With one hand, the boy swung a war club over his head and charged her. The Flint girl, whose name she couldn't recall, followed him swinging an axe...and Chipmunk Teeth leaped forward with a stiletto clutched in her fist. The other two girls stood by with stunned expressions. The pretty little girl that she'd had such high hopes for had a vague sweet smile on her face.

22

The child's scream momentarily froze Koracoo in her tracks; then as recognition filtered through her shock, she shouted, "*Odion!*"

Her feet kicked up puffs of snow behind her as she rounded a clump of brush and dashed headlong toward the snow-bright clearing ahead, where dark patches—people—moved against the white. CorpseEye had gone fiery in her grip, leading her on.

"Koracoo?" Sindak called. "Wait! This could be a trap!"

She didn't even slow.

An eerie chorus of children's screams rang through the night, possessing a terrifying animalistic rage—pure emotion without reason or remorse.

She charged across the clearing toward where the children stood, calling, "Odion? Odion, answer me! Are you all right?"

When she was twenty paces away, her son turned to look at her. He blinked as though awakening from a dream and seeing her for the first time. Even in the soft moonlight, she could tell that he was drenched in blood. It covered his face and cape as though poured over his head. His left arm was hanging limply at his side, but in his right hand, he carried a war club clenched in his fist. The expression on his face wasn't that of a child, but of a victorious warrior standing over the dead body of the man who'd killed his family.

Baji stood beside him with a dripping axe, and Zateri stood two paces away with a stiletto. A short distance away were two other girls. She did not know them. One was standing. The other, younger, lay on her side curled in the snow. She had a finger tucked in her mouth, sucking it as an infant would.

In a shaking voice, Odion called, "Mother, she —she was trying to escape. We had to stop her!"

Koracoo dropped to her knees in the snow, laid CorpseEye on the ground, and—careful of his wounded shoulder—enfolded Odion in her arms. "Thank the gods you're all right."

"We couldn't let her escape, Mother," he repeated as though explaining. "She threatened to witch us. She was going to get away."

"She would have just bought more children," Baji said with unnerving calm, but as she lowered her hand, the bloody axe toppled into the snow, and tears slid down her cheeks. "We had to end it."

"Mother, I think my shoulder's broken."

Koracoo gently probed the injury with her fingers. His collarbone had been snapped, but it hadn't broken through the skin, which would protect him from the evil Spirits who fed on such wounds. "You're going to be all right, Odion, though it's going to be agony for a while. Is anyone else hurt?"

Baji and Zateri shook their heads; then they all turned and looked at the little girl curled in the snow. Her long black hair feathered across the snow. "When Odion hit the old woman in the spine and flattened her in the snow, something happened to Conkesema," the older Dawnland girl said. "She collapsed like her feet had been knocked out from under her."

"Is she your sister?"

"She's my cousin. I'm Auma."

Sindak and Towa halted a few paces away, and Towa said, "What happened?"

Sindak softly replied, "I can't tell."

Koracoo's gaze moved to the body. Had it not been for the broken gorget around her neck, the mutilated corpse would have been unrecognizable.

The children must have kept striking her long after she was dead.

Odion suddenly shoved away to stare Koracoo in the eyes. "Mother, we left Wrass. He's hurt. We have to hurry. We have to go get him before the warriors find him!" He broke into a run, heading up the hill.

"Her warriors are dead, Odion," she called after him. "They can't hurt anyone now."

"All of them? Some must have escaped." He stopped long enough to hear her answer.

"A few escaped, but I think they're long gone."

Odion took a deep halting breath, then exhaled the words, "Maybe, but maybe not. They may still be out there. We have to find Wrass. I have to know he's safe." He charged up the hill again.

As Koracoo rose to her feet, Sindak walked to stand over Gannajero. For a time, he just frowned; then he bent and pulled the broken gorget over her head. "Where's the other half?"

"I don't know, but we'd better find it," Towa said. "Chief Atotarho will want it." Towa kneeled on the opposite side of the body and began brushing at the snow, searching for it.

"Forget it," Koracoo said. "There's no time. Towa, I want you to get back to camp as soon as you can. Take Cord and Gonda and go find Wakdanek. Wait for us along the eastern shore. We'll meet you."

"But, Koracoo, that gorget belongs to the Wolf Clan. If I don't return it, Atotarho—"

"Once I start asking questions the last thing your chief will be worried about is the gorget. Go on. Conkesema needs her father far more urgently than you need a broken piece of shell."

Towa looked at Conkesema lying in the snow. Her sweet face looked oddly happy. "You're right." He sprinted away.

Sindak turned to Koracoo. "And what of me, War Chief?" Locks of his black hair had come loose from their tie and danced around his beaked face in the breeze. He kept glancing at Baji and Zateri, then at the old woman's body, clearly shocked by what the children had done.

Koracoo used CorpseEye to gesture to Sindak's wounded shoulder. "I need you to help me get the children back to camp. Can you carry CorpseEye?"

An expression of awe creased his face. "Yes." He extended his hand, and she placed the club in it. Sindak drew it back as though he'd just grasped hold of a deadly serpent.

When Koracoo kneeled at Conkesema's side, the child didn't even blink. She just sucked her finger and stared blankly at the night sky. "I'm slipping my arms under you," Koracoo announced. As she lifted her, the girl let out a faint whimper. "Everything's all right. I'm going to take you to your father."

Koracoo turned. "All right, let's all follow Odion."

23

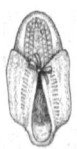

The screams and shouts had stopped, but Odion still had not returned, and Wrass was shaking badly, more afraid than he'd ever been in his life.

If she killed Odion, there's nothing left, no hope...

"Wrass?"

He went stone still. The faint call seemed to swirl around on Wind Mother's breath, like a distant echo bouncing through the trees.

He pulled his bowstring tighter and tried not to move.

There was something out there. An odd tang rode the wind, like the tang of carrion. His hands clenched on the nocked bow as his gaze swept the trees and brush that fringed the clearing. If his first shot missed, he'd never be able to nock a second arrow fast enough to defend himself. Which meant his first arrow had to fly true. He braced his shaking arms on his drawn-up knees.

He'd dragged himself down the hill to the edge of the trees to get away from the sounds and small jerks Dakion's body continued to make. He was almost invisible here. If he could...

He twisted around when something wavered in the darkness to his left.

Like great black wings flapping, the man's cape billowed around him when he walked out of the forest. He stopped five paces away, his back to the snow-blanketed clearing, and lightly clasped his hands before him. The man carried no weapons. The old copper beads that ringed the neck of his cape had turned blue-green from lack of polishing. The man's face, as white and luminescent as seashell in the gloom, flashed when he cocked his head to study Wrass.

Wrass whispered in awe, "You...you're real. When I saw you on the river I thought you were just a figment of my fever. Are you...? You're Shag-oniyoh, aren't you?"

The man stepped closer, and as he kneeled in front of Wrass, shining strands of his fine hair blew across his cheeks like moonlit spiderwebs.

In an eerily quiet voice, he asked, "Do you recall what I told you that night on the river?"

Wrass licked his cracked lips. "About Elder

Brother Sun blackening his face with the soot of the dying world?"

The man nodded, but it was such a subtle gesture, Wrass almost missed it.

"Yes, I remember. Why?"

"I made you a promise."

Wrass had to think about it. "You said that I would know the one who is to come. At the end of the world. The Human False Face who will don the cape of white clouds and ride the winds of destruction..."

Wrass stopped when the man turned, lifted a hand, and pointed to the opposite side of the clearing, where a boy ran across the snow. He was holding his left arm, running as hard as he could, calling, *"Wrass? Wrass, are you all right?"*

A strange light-headed sensation came over Wrass. In awe, he whispered, "Are you sure?"

The man smiled, but it was a sad smile, filled with loss and longing, as though he could see the way ahead, and it was not an easy path. Softly, he said, "Help him, if you can."

The man's cape flared as he rose to his feet and walked away into the trees. In moments, he was gone, swallowed by the darkness.

Odion charged straight for the last place he'd seen Wrass, and when Wrass wasn't there, he panicked. He spun around and cried, *"Wrass! Wrass, where are you?"*

Two adults and three children followed a little way behind Odion.

One of the adults seemed to be carrying something.

"I'm down here, Odion!" he shouted back. "Near the trees!" People started running toward him, but Odion was in the lead, his legs pumping, trying hard to get to Wrass first.

24
ODION

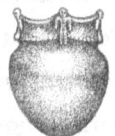

I lie on the packs with Gitchi curled against me. The puppy's head is healing, though he still whimpers in his sleep. I pet his fur gently and watch Wakdanek on the opposite side of the canoe. He rocks Conkesema in his arms and whispers in her ear. She hasn't spoken or taken her eyes from him since we found him waiting along the riverbank with Hehaka and Tutelo. The little girl has one hand twined in Wakdanek's shirt sleeve, as though she'll never let go.

The night is quiet and cold. Mist hovers low over the river, and I imagine that if I just reach out I can touch it. Along the banks, it creeps among the tree trunks like ghostly white arms.

Gitchi shifts and props his nose on my hand. "Everything's all right now," I murmur. "We're going home."

Ahead of us on the water, Mother and War Chief Cord paddle against the current, trying to stay close to shore. In the middle of their canoe, Zateri and Baji sit side by side with their arms around each other, talking. I don't know where Tutelo and Auma are. They must be sleeping in the bottom of Mother's canoe.

Wakdanek has told us that he will be leaving us tomorrow, taking Conkesema and Auma back to find whatever remains of their families. After that, War Chief Cord will take Baji away with him to Flint country, while Mother and the rest of us head for Atotarho Village to make sure that Zateri and Hehaka make it home. Finally, Mother will lead the way to Bur Oak Village, where, hopefully, we will find the last survivors of Yellowtail Village. As I gaze at Zateri and Baji, my heart aches. I miss them already. Over the past moon, our souls have woven them-selves together into a fine tight weave. We are part of each other. I'll be ripped apart when they go home.

My gaze shifts to Father, who paddles in the bow of our canoe while Towa steers the canoe from the rear. Sindak and Hehaka sleep on the packs just in front of me, and Wrass sits in front of them. Every time I turn, I find Wrass watching me with glistening eyes.

I shift my aching shoulder. Wakdanek bandaged it and made me a sling, but it hurts badly. Father says he doesn't know if I'll have the full use of it when it heals. Right now, I don't care. I'm alive. So are my friends.

Gitchi growls in his sleep, and his feet twitch. I whisper, "You're safe, boy. You don't have to run anymore."

And for the first time in over a moon, I think maybe I can stop running, too.

Father turns and frowns at me for several moments; then he ships his paddle and carefully climbs over the packs and around sleeping people to get to me. The lines at the corners of his eyes crinkle as he scans my face. "You are a man now, Son. A warrior," he says with pride in his voice. "There's something I want to give you."

"What is it, Father?" I sit up straight.

Father pulls a False Face gorget from around his throat and drapes it over my head.

In awe, I say, "This looks just like the one that Towa—"

"It's not the same. It's just a copy, but it has Power. I've felt it. I want you to have it. Perhaps it will protect you in the days to come."

Father smiles again, then makes his way back to the bow and picks up his paddle.

I reach down to trace the stars with my fingers. When I look at Wrass, he's still staring at me. I nod to him.

He nods back and calls, "I didn't think you'd get that so soon."

"What do you mean?"

"Nothing." He shakes his head. "It's beautiful."

A strange sensation filters through me. It is as though I have just awakened from a long sleep and discovered that it is winter and the trees are bare and coated with snow, and I realize I am cold and very tired.

Wrass' gaze shifts to Baji and Zateri. They are talking and smiling. A sad smile creases his face, and my heart aches. Wrass must feel the same sense of loss that I do, dreading the moment when our friends go away. I don't even want to think about it.

For now, I'm safe. They're still here. We're still together.

I curl my body around Gitchi and watch the endless trees pass by.

25

As they were escorted across the village by Nesi and twenty warriors with war clubs, Odion's gaze drifted over the broad plaza. Zateri walked close beside him. She kept licking her lips and staring around as though this was just another dream, and it might disappear at any instant. Ahead of him, Koracoo and Gonda walked, and behind him, Hehaka clung onto Towa's cape as though he feared he was about to be eaten alive. Sindak had insisted upon staying outside to guard Tutelo and Wrass until they returned.

The four longhouses were arranged in a rough oval around the plaza. Odion studied them. This was a huge village, perhaps the largest village anywhere on earth. On the eastern side, near the forty-hand-tall palisade wall, four smaller clan houses and another house, probably the prisoners' house, stood. The magnificent longhouses—surely the biggest ever built—were constructed of pole frames and covered with slippery elm bark. The house they walked toward stretched over eight hundred hands long and forty wide. The others were shorter, two or three hundred hands long, but still stunning. The arched roofs soared over fifty hands high.

Laughing children raced by, followed by a pack of dogs wagging their tails. Zateri craned her neck, trying to see faces, but the group of warriors was packed too tightly around them. Odion could barely glimpse eyes. People began to run across the plaza, coalescing into a large crowd. They surrounded the warriors, calling questions, trying to see who was being protected inside the circle.

"Is that Zateri?" a woman cried. "*Zateri?*"

"Aunt Dinaga! I'm here, I'm right here!"

"Thank the Spirits, you're all right! We had feared the worst."

Aunt Dinaga tried to force her way into the warriors' circle to get to Zateri, but War Chief Nesi shouted, "Stay back! The chief wishes to speak with them first. You can all talk after the chief is finished."

Aunt Dinaga faded back with a heartbroken expression on her face. Then the grumbling began. People shouted curses at Koracoo and Gonda.

Someone threw a rock at Gonda. He ducked and glared.

Zateri whispered, "Odion, stay very close to me. I won't let *anyone* hurt you." She grabbed his hand and held onto it, dragging him forward.

The big war chief, Nesi, must have sensed that the mood was changing. He picked up his pace and led them forward at a run.

"Towa!" a man yelled from the right, and Odion glimpsed the man running at the edge of the warriors. He had seen perhaps thirty-five summers and had gray-speckled long hair. "Are you all right?"

Towa lifted a hand, and called, "I'm fine, Father! I'll see you soon. Tell Sindak's parents he is well, also."

"I will!"

When they approached her longhouse, tears filled Zateri's eyes.

Odion asked, "Are you all right?"

"Yes, I just never thought I'd see home again." Her gaze lifted to the two massive log pillars carved with faces and painted in rich shades of red, blue, black, and pure white that stood outside the door. "All of my life, every summer, I've watched people repaint the Faces that protect our longhouse. They are like old friends looking down upon me."

She reached out as though she longed to touch them, to speak with their Spirits, but Nesi drew back the leather curtain that held in the longhouse warmth and ordered, "Hurry. Get inside before I have a riot to put down."

As Mother and Father passed War Chief Nesi, they exchanged threatening glances, and Odion wondered if they'd met before. Perhaps in battle?

Odion ducked into the longhouse still holding Zateri's hand, and Nesi said, "Lonkol, I want half of the warriors guarding this end of the house, and other half stationed at the opposite end."

"Yes, Nesi."

Feet pounded the frozen ground as men trotted away. Odion blinked, trying to rush his eyes into adjusting to the firelit darkness. He'd been staring at brilliant sunlight reflecting from snow for forty-three days. It would likely take a while to adjust.

All he could see now were the forty fires that burned down the length of the house. They resembled a chain of amber beads. As his vision began to clear, he looked up. High over his head, blue wood smoke crept along the ceiling until it was sucked out through the smoke holes. Cornstalks, vines of squashes, and beans, as well as whole sunflowers hung from the rafters, curing in the rising smoke. The sudden warmth made him shiver.

"Grandmother?" Zateri called, her voice breaking. "Mother?"

She released Odion's hand and lunged forward to run down the length of the house, but Nesi grabbed her arm as she passed him. "Stay here. Your father is coming." Scars crisscrossed his face like thick white worms. They writhed when he glowered at her.

"But, Nesi, I live here. Why can't I go look for Mother?"

"Ask your father when he arrives."

Zateri swallowed her hope and returned to stand beside Odion. "Something's wrong," she whispered.

"It may be nothing. Don't worry yet."

His gaze drifted, searching the low shelves stuffed with pots, baskets, and personal belongings, and the sleeping benches that lined the walls above them. Bark partitions separated each family's space, providing some privacy. And far away, down at the end of the house, people were gathered. Soft voices echoed.

Koracoo, Gonda, and Towa moved closer together and spoke in whispers. Their expressions made Odion's belly knot up.

"Where's our father?" Hehaka whispered as he edged forward to stand beside Zateri. Fear tensed his triangular face, and his bat nose wriggled as he smelled the air.

Zateri balled her fists. "I don't know. Probably down there."

"What's he doing?"

For a long moment the question didn't make

sense. The gathering was obviously a village council meeting. Then it occurred to Odion that Hehaka had not been raised in a longhouse or even in a village.

He'd spent his entire life moving from camp to camp with a small party of outcast warriors. He knew nothing of village life.

Zateri explained, "Each clan has its own council, but the village also has one big council of clan elders. This is the village council."

Hehaka's small black eyes narrowed. "I don't like this. I don't want to be here. Who are the people standing on the right?"

"Those are the Speakers. Different groups elect one person to communicate their decisions. There is a Speaker for the Women, a Speaker for the Warriors, each clan has a Speaker, and there are many more."

Hehaka folded his arms beneath his cape, looking worried and confused.

"Don't worry, you'll learn quickly. I'll help you. You...you're my brother."

An old man with a crooked body broke away from the group and hobbled toward them. Zateri took a deep breath.

"Is that your father?" Odion asked.

"Yes. I'm not sure how to feel."

She had learned things about her father that no child should know. After hearing that he'd sold his younger sister and brother when they'd seen eight summers, her eyes probably saw him differently.

"No matter what he's done, he's still your father, Zateri," Odion said.

"I know." Her gaze clung to him.

He must have seen over fifty summers. As he came closer, Odion saw that he had braided rattlesnake skins into his gray-streaked black hair, then coiled it into a bun at the base of his head and secured it with a wooden comb. The style gave his narrow face a starved look. He wore a beautiful black cape covered with circlets cut from human skulls.

Gonda said to Koracoo, "Here it comes."

Koracoo straightened and squared her shoulders, as though anticipating a fight. "Towa, are you ready?"

"Yes," he responded softly. In the firelight, Odion saw his handsome face go hard.

Chief Atotarho stopped two paces away, kneeled, and opened his arms. "Zateri, I've missed you so much."

She let out a small incoherent cry and threw herself into his arms, crying, "Father, I'm so glad to be home." The last word turned into a high-pitched wail.

The chief crushed her against his chest and kissed her hair. "Forgive me for everything you've gone through," he said. "I would have gone through it for you, if I could have."

"It's all right," she sobbed. "I'm home now. Where's Mother?"

He pushed her back to look into her eyes. "She'll be here soon."

At the far end of the longhouse, the council members began leaving. The curtain lifted over and over, allowing in long rectangles of sunlight. A handful of people remained. They stood like dark pillars, watching.

Chief Atotarho gently touched Zateri's cheek and rose to face Koracoo. She spread her feet.

The chief asked, "She's dead?"

"Yes."

Atotarho briefly closed his eyes, as though the news grieved him.

Koracoo said, "I assume you do not want to speak further in front of the children."

Atotarho opened his eyes. "I must. After what they've been through, they deserve to know the truth."

Koracoo gave him a suspicious look. The blue buffalo painted in the middle of her red cape seemed to walk with her uneasy movements. Finally, she nodded. "Very well."

Atotarho put a hand on Zateri's shoulder. "Someday Zateri will lead this clan, and perhaps this nation. The things she is about to hear may help her do that." He looked down at Zateri, and his eyes tightened. "But they will not be easy for you. Do you understand?"

She glanced at Koracoo's distrustful expression, then at Odion, and finally looked back at her father. "Yes."

Atotarho had not asked a single question about Hehaka, and Odion saw Hehaka fidgeting, perhaps longing to be held as Zateri had been, or just simply to be acknowledged. The chief stared only at Koracoo.

"You must have many questions, War Chief. Ask. I will answer, if I can."

With only the barest hesitation, Koracoo said, "You used your own daughter as bait. Why?"

A swallow went down Atotarho's throat. "It had to end. I had to stop her. It was the only way I knew."

It was as though the earth beneath Odion's feet had suddenly turned to mud and was sucking him down into the dark underworlds. *It's true, then. Hallowed Ancestors, he sold Zateri...*

Mother tilted her head to stare at Atotarho, and it was like Eagle spying Mouse. Her intent was deadly. "And you lied to us."

"You mean about what happened to my brother and sister. I—"

"Is it true that you sold them when they'd seen only eight summers?" Gonda demanded to know. His short black hair glistened in the firelight.

"Yes." Atotarho's voice was so low, we almost couldn't hear it. "But there's much more to the story."

"So, she didn't tell us everything?" Koracoo asked.

A brief flicker of panic touched Atotarho's expression, but it vanished quickly. Cautiously, he asked, "What did she tell you?"

Koracoo didn't move a muscle. She didn't blink. She just stared at the chief with burning eyes.

Atotarho looked away. "Well, it doesn't matter what she told you." He smoothed a hand over Zateri's hair. "It started when Jonodak—that was her name—had seen eight summers."

The circlets of skull that decorated his black cape flashed as he opened his palms to Koracoo. "She hurt her twin brother first. They'd been inseparable. No one would have ever—"

"How did she hurt him?"

Atotarho pulled his hands back. Koracoo's interruption was an insult to the chief. If she had been a Hills warrior she'd probably be dead in a less than a handful of heartbeats.

But Atotarho just replied, "One night the entire longhouse was awakened by screams. When I rushed to my younger brother's bed, I found him sitting up, covered in blood. She was crouched beside him with a sharp chert flake in her hand, smiling. She'd sliced his throat. Fortunately she'd missed the big artery. We cared for him, and eventually returned to our blankets. Just before dawn the screams started again. She had apparently carried a rock to bed with her. She must have hidden it somewhere. She'd slammed it into her brother's face."

"Was he disfigured?"

Was Koracoo thinking about Tutelo's descriptions of Shagoniyoh and his crooked nose? Odion found himself breathlessly waiting for the chief's answer.

"Yes. Our village Healers tried to set the bones, but it was impossible. She'd crushed them." Atotarho ran a hand over his face as though he still couldn't believe it had happened. "A few days later, Jonodak attacked three other children. Two died from their wounds.

"One was the grandson of a clan elder." He paused as if trying to remember, then said, "His name was Skaneat. He'd seen only four summers."

No one said anything. But Odion noticed that Zateri was breathing hard.

"Why both of them?" Koracoo asked in a low menacing voice.

Atotarho seemed confused at first; then his jaw clenched. "It wasn't my decision. I was Towa's age, a warrior of some repute. I followed the orders of the council of elders. It tore my souls apart. You cannot possibly imagine what it was like..." His voice died as though he couldn't continue. "You know the requirements of the Law of Retribution."

Koracoo's face slackened, and she saw Towa's eyes suddenly go wide in understanding. Hehaka was gazing from one person to the next in confusion.

The chief gazed down at his daughter. "Do you understand, Zateri?"

"Yes, Father. Murder is the worst crime. Clans have a right to demand retribution."

Gonda nodded. "Murder places an absolute obligation on the relatives of the dead to avenge the murder. They may demand reparations, exotic trade goods, finely tanned beaver robes, maybe food. They may also claim the life of the murderer, or the life of another member of his clan."

Koracoo said, "Then the families of the murdered children claimed the lives of both your sister and her twin brother?"

Atotarho bowed his head. "They did. The Wolf Clan council ordered me to carry out the duty, but I was too much of a coward to do it. I tried. I took them out into the forest. I was a warrior. I should have been able to carry out the order without question."

Towa silently walked forward, and his cape

swung around his long legs. "You sold them and told the village elders that you'd killed them?"

Shame filled the chief's eyes. "There is a very important lesson here, my daughter. Never, *never* disobey your clan elders. It's because of my cowardice that Jonodak became a monster."

A log broke in the fire, and sparks crackled and whirled upward toward the smoke holes.

"When did the elders discover your deceit?" Gonda asked.

"There had always been rumors. Over the long summers, many young women showed up here claiming to be her. But the elders didn't know for certain until seven summers ago. A Trader came through saying that he'd met an insane woman who said she was the rightful matron of the Wolf Clan. Everyone laughed. Then three moons later an outcast warrior trotted in with captive children for sale. He said he'd bought them from Jonodak, who he said was now calling herself...well, you know that part."

"Your clan must have been unhappy," Koracoo said.

A pained smile came to the chief's face. "The dead children's clans were livid. They claimed the life of my son." He gestured weakly to Hehaka, and Hehaka's mouth fell open. "They ordered me to kill him, then to finish the job and kill Jonodak, or they threatened to claim the life of my mother, or perhaps my grandmother. I hired men. They told me they'd killed her and my son. The clans were satisfied. I didn't know until much later that Hehaka—"

"You never came for me," Hehaka cried in a plaintive voice. "I waited."

Atotarho didn't look at him. He stared straight at Koracoo with his jaw clenched.

Koracoo asked, "Why did you use Zateri?"

The chief's mouth trembled. "I knew she was the only thing that might draw Jonodak out. Zateri was Jonodak's only competition for the leadership of Atotarho Village. I thought if I could capture my sister and kill her for her crimes...I never thought...I mean it never occurred to me that she might actually capture Zateri."

Zateri stared up at her father with her eyes narrowed, clearly not sure she believed him.

Koracoo glanced at Zateri, then propped her hands on her hips. Her red cape flared out, pulling the blue buffalo tight across the middle of her chest. "We heard a different story about Hehaka."

The chief shrugged. "I'm sure you did." He turned to Towa. "I assume you brought the clan's sacred gorget back?"

Towa tugged the leather thong over his head and extended the broken gorget. "Your sister broke it. We couldn't find the other half in the snow."

Atotarho grasped the gorget and angrily pulled

it from Towa's fingers. As he frowned at the broken shell, he said, "I'll dispatch someone to see if he can find the other half."

"Very well."

Atotarho hesitated before he asked, "Did you bury her?"

Koracoo vented a low laugh, and the chief's eyes immediately lifted and slitted.

She said, "No. In fact, we made certain her soul will be wandering the earth forever. We left her for the wolves to tear to pieces and scatter far and wide."

Hehaka let out a pathetic whimper, turned, and ran out of the longhouse. No one went after him.

A small shudder passed through Zateri. Odion suspected he knew why. For the rest of his life, he would fear that the old woman's ghost was waiting out in the forest. Watching him. Always about to catch him again. Zateri must be feeling something similar.

Gonda stood with his feet braced and his fists at his sides. To his right, around the fire, dishes were neatly stacked. The bowls were made from human skulls and the spoons from ground and polished human leg bones. Gonda seemed to be looking at them; then his gaze shifted to human finger-bone bracelets that encircled Atotarho's wrists, and disdain twisted his face. All the people in this village seemed to wear jewelry and eat from dishes made of human beings.

Voices echoed, and Zateri turned. At the far end of the longhouse, the elders appeared impatient. They kept looking at Atotarho and whispering behind their hands.

Koracoo said, "You treated Hehaka badly."

Atotarho's expression turned cold. As he tilted his head, the rattlesnake skins woven into his graying black hair shimmered. "I've heard he is a monster. I fear he may be another Jonodak. Besides, how long do you think he has to live? It may be my duty to kill him in the near future."

A faint cold smile turned Koracoo's lips. To Gonda, she said, "Well, that was an interesting story."

"Yes. Very entertaining. Clean. Every detail carefully worked through."

Koracoo tipped her head to the group of elders. "Is all of this for Zateri's benefit? Or the people down there?"

Atotarho made an airy gesture with his hand, and his finger-bone bracelets rattled. "I don't care if you believe me."

Koracoo said, "Really? Then what are they waiting for?"

Atotarho eyed her malevolently, and Gonda's right fist flexed.

"I have been...mistaken...in the past," the chief

explained. "They rightly wish to be assured that she is truly dead this time."

"She is."

Atotarho slipped the broken gorget around his neck and adjusted it over his cape. "I am grateful to you for bringing my children home. You are under my protection until you pass beyond the boundaries of Hills Country. At that point, War Chief, you and your friends are no longer my allies. You will be my enemies again."

Koracoo's red cape swayed as she lowered her hands to her sides. "Yes. We will be."

Atotarho dipped his head in a nod and turned to Zateri. "Come, my daughter. The elders wish to hear your tale."

She clenched her fists and turned to Odion. For a few moments, they just stared at each other with their hearts breaking; then Odion walked forward, wrapped his good arm around her, and hugged her with all the strength in his body. "I will never, *never,* forget you, Zateri. If you ever need me, send word. I will be here as fast as I can."

Crying, she answered, "I love you, Odion. I always will."

A strand of her black hair had caught on his sleeve and pulled free. He twined his fingers around it, keeping it. In the future, when he was scared or desperate, he wanted to be able to touch her, to remind himself that she'd been real.

Atotarho put a hand on Zateri's shoulder and tugged them apart. "We must let our guests leave, Zateri. They have a long way to go before Elder Brother Sun sets."

"I know, Father."

As she walked away at Atotarho's side, Zateri turned several times to look back at Odion.

Koracoo continued to stare down the length of the longhouse at the assembled elders. Odion couldn't read her expression. It seemed to be a mixture of curiosity and hatred. At last, she said, "Let's go," and strode for the door curtain.

EPILOGUE
ODION

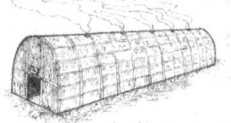

Night is falling, draping the forest with gray velvet shadows. Wrass keeps glancing at me from where he walks at my side, and I wonder if he feels the same dread I do. Like a sleeping monster, terror lives just behind my eyes. Breathing deep, dreaming.

I focus on the trail ahead, where Tutelo trudges with her head down, following Mother and Father. Far in the distance, Gitchi trots, scouting the way. The scent of damp trees and earth is strong.

"We're on our way home, Odion," Wrass says. "Everything is going to be all right." He reaches out to touch my shoulder.

I give him a vague smile and nod. The sound of my friend's voice, the touch of his hand, softly stir the ashes in my heart—the ashes of the days before the attack on Yellowtail Village. A sad hunger for them fills my chest.

"Our relatives will be waiting for us. They'll be so happy to see us. There will be feasting and dancing. Songs will fill the air. There will be great joy."

He sounds so happy.

Under the spell of Wrass' voice, the darkening forest fades and the moons roll away, leaving us racing across the plaza together in a long-gone summer. As his light grip on my shoulder tightens, I hear old half-forgotten laughter, see the sun glinting on the faces of the other racing boys, and watch our spears, cast almost at once, sail through the air toward the stone that careens across a plaza that is no more. There is the far-off barking of dogs in the autumn-hued trees and the smell of roasting corn. Old friends come marching back laughing as though they have not been dead these many moons, and the whisper and fragrance that is Grandmother Jigon-saseh's cape carries on the wind. Behind it all rests a sense of security and warmth, a false knowledge that tomorrow will bring the same happiness today brought.

"Odion?" Wrass calls, breaking the spell. He leans forward to make me look at him. Concern lines his hawkish face. "Please talk to me."

"I'm all right, Wrass," I say. "I just miss them. Baji and Zateri."

His brows lower as though he's grieving, too.

There are so many other children who are slaves, lost, and desperate to get home. I must never let myself forget that, but I must also start trying to look ahead. No man can survive if he is always looking backward.

Wrass playfully bumps my shoulder and leans against me for a few awkward steps. It makes me smile. Having him close is like cool water on a fevered wound. I feel safe for the first time since I lost sight of Zateri.

"I miss them, too. But we'll see them again. You know that, don't you?"

Neither of us speaks of Hehaka. He was never one of us. Never one of the trusted few for whom we would have willingly given our lives.

"I know we will," I whisper. But I'm lying, and he seems to know it.

"We *will*," he answers in a strong voice, as though the desperate wanting alone will make it come true. "I'm sure of it, Odion."

I want to believe him, but we are at war with everyone around us—and we are men now. Warriors. Deep inside me, I fear that someday I may be ordered to attack their villages. I will refuse, of course...and then my clan will accuse me of treason. What will I do? Has Wrass thought of these things? Is he thinking them even now? The sound of our moccasins hitting the trail is faint, barely there.

"I had a strange dream last night, Wrass," I abruptly confess. "It scared me."

He grips my shoulder and forces me to stop walking. His stare seems to pierce my heart. "What dream?"

I hesitate. "It's many summers from now. You and I are together. We're standing in a clearing surrounded by Mountain warriors."

His fists clench. "Go on."

I lift my hand and gesture futilely. "It's...bizarre. It's the middle of the day, bright, too bright. I can't feel my body, just the air cooling as the color suddenly leaches from the forest, leaving the land gray and shimmery. It must be summer, because hundreds of butterflies settle into the grass at my feet, and the world goes strangely quiet. You call my name and point, and my gaze moves to the west, where I see a black cloud rising from the depths of Skanodario Lake. It slithers along the horizon like Horned Serpent in the Beginning Time. Elder Brother Sun seems frightened. His blazing face begins to darken, and I know he is about to turn his back on the world and flee, leaving us all to die in the cold blackness." Shivering racks my body, as though the end of the world has already crept into my veins. I force myself to stop. "I feel so empty, Wrass, like an old husk."

In a deathly quiet voice, he says, *"We are all husks, Odion, flayed from the soil of fire and blood. This won't be over for any of us until the Great Face shakes the World Tree. Then, when Elder Brother Sun blackens his face with the soot of the dying world, the judgment will take place."*

My heart seems to stop. I feel as though I'm floating in a vast silent sea. "The judgment?" I whisper. "That's what it feels like. Where did you hear that?"

Wrass looks away, up the trail, and expels a breath before he answers, "It's something Shagoniyoh told me."

"What?" I ask breathlessly. "When?"

"On the river. I was fevered. It may have just been a dream, but I think it was real."

My gaze instinctively scans the twilight forest, searching for him, praying to see a shred of his wind-blown cape or hear his deep voice call my name. There is only the distant howling of wolves.

"Gods, Wrass, I pray that means he will be there with me at the end."

Wrass swallows hard. "I don't know if he'll be there. He didn't tell me." His gaze shifts to the forest, examining the shadows as though he, too, longs to glimpse the Forest Spirit. When he finally turns back to me, his expression is somber, serious. In a very soft voice, he vows, "But *I* will be there. I promise you on my life, I will be right at your side."

Our gazes lock and hold.

Without warning, tears well in my eyes and roll slowly down my cheeks. Wrass says nothing. He just walks forward and wraps his arm around me, holding me so tightly he shakes. Only Wrass, who shares the sunny lost days of my boyhood as well as my memories of the past few moons, can understand.

All I want are the sheltering walls of a warm longhouse, a corner in which to hide and hurt, enough peace to allow me to heal.

In my ear, Wrass says again, "We're going home, Odion. Everything is going to be all right."

I let out a breath and high above me see a dove flapping through the slate-colored sky, its wings sleek in the last gleam of day. I swear, for just a moment...I believe him.

A LOOK AT BOOK FIVE:
THE BROKEN LAND

Twelve summers after the events of *People of the Longhouse* and *The Dawn Country*, the Iroquois nations remain locked in bitter warfare. Atotarho, the cannibal sorcerer who leads the People of the Hills, schemes to set into motion a cataclysmic battle that threatens to destroy the Iroquoian world. His warriors spread fear and death wherever they go, taking captives and burning villages to the ground.

Only five people are brave enough to challenge Atotarho. Odion, Wrass, Tutelo, Baji, and Zateri, kidnapped as children and sold into slavery, are now grown, and they have forged a desperate alliance that just might be strong enough to stop the madman.

Dive into this riveting tale of bravery, sacrifice, and the enduring spirit of survival.

AVAILABLE JULY 2024

ABOUT W. MICHAEL GEAR

W. Michael Gear is a *New York Times, USA Today,* and international bestselling author of sixty novels. With close to eighteen million copies of his books in print worldwide, his work has been translated into twenty-nine languages.

Gear has been inducted into the Western Writers Hall of Fame and the Colorado Authors' Hall of Fame—as well as won the Owen Wister Award, the Golden Spur Award, and the International Book Award for both Science Fiction and Action Suspense Fiction. He is also the recipient of the Frank Waters Award for lifetime contributions to Western writing.

Gear's work, inspired by anthropology and archaeology, is multilayered and has been called compelling, insidiously realistic, and masterful. Currently, he lives in northwestern Wyoming with his award-winning wife and co-author, Kathleen O'Neal Gear, and a charming sheltie named, Jake.

ABOUT KATHLEEN O'NEAL GEAR

Kathleen O'Neal Gear is a *New York Times* bestselling author of fifty-seven books and a national award-winning archaeologist. The U.S. Department of the Interior has awarded her two Special Achievement awards for outstanding management of America's cultural resources.

In 2015 the United States Congress honored her with a Certificate of Special Congressional Recognition, and the California State Legislature passed Joint Member Resolution #117 saying, "The contributions of Kathleen O'Neal Gear to the fields of history, archaeology, and writing have been invaluable..."

In 2021 she received the Owen Wister Award for lifetime contributions to western literature, and in 2023 received the Frank Waters Award for "a body of work representing excellence in writing and storytelling that embodies the spirit of the American West."

PLACES TO VISIT

There are many places in the United States and Canada that bring Iroquois culture to life. Some of our favorites are listed below. We encourage you to visit them. Each makes a great family trip.

The Iroquois Indian Museum
    Howes Cave, New York
    Phone: 518-296-8949
    www.iroquoismuseum.org

Ganondagan State Historic Site
    Victor, New York
    Phone: 585-742-1690
    www.ganondagan.org

Sainte-Marie among the Hurons

Midland, Ontario, Canada
Phone: 705-526-7838
www.saintemarieamongthehurons.on.ca

SELECTED BIBLIOGRAPHY

Bruchac, Joseph. *Iroquois Stories: Heroes and Heroines, Monsters and Magic*. Freedom, Calif.: The Crossing Press, 1985.

Calloway, Colin G. *The Western Abenakis of Vermont, 1600-1800*. Norman: University of Oklahoma Press, 1990.

Custer, Jay F. *Delaware Prehistoric Archaeology: An Ecological Approach*. Cranberry, N.J.: Associated University Presses, 1984.

Dye, David H. *War Paths, Peace Paths: An Archaeology of Cooperation and Conflict in Native Eastern North America*. Lanham, Md.: AltaMira Press, 2009.

Ellis, Chris J., and Neal Ferris, eds. *The Archaeology of Southern Ontario to A.D. 1650*. London, Ontario, Canada: Occasional Papers of the London Chapter, OAS Number 5, 1990.

Elm, Demus, and Harvey Antone. *The Oneida Creation Story*. Lincoln: University of Nebraska, 2000.

Englebrecht, William. *Iroquoia: The Development of a Native World*. Syracuse: Syracuse University Press, 2003.

Fagan, Brian M. *Ancient North America: The Archaeology of a Continent*, 4th ed. London: Thames and Hudson Press, 2005.

Fenton, William N. *The False Faces of the Iroquois*. Norman: University of Oklahoma Press, 1987.

—. *The Iroquois Eagle Dance: An Offshoot of the Calumet Dance*. Syracuse: Syracuse University Press, 1991.

—. *The Roll Call of the Iroquois Chiefs: A Study of a Mnemonic Cane from the Six Nations Reserve*. Bulletin No. 30. Cranbrook Institute of Science, Bloomfield Hills, Mich.: 1950.

Foster, Steven and James A. Duke. *Eastern/Central Medicinal*

Plants. The Peterson Guides Series. Boston: Houghton Mifflin Company, 1990.

Hart, John P., and Christina B. Reith. *Northeast Subsistence-Settlement Change: AD 700-1300.* Bulletin 496. Albany: New York State Museum, 2002.

Herrick, James W. *Iroquois Medical Botany.* Syracuse: Syracuse University Press, 1995.

Jennings, Francis. *The Ambiguous Iroquois Empire.* New York: W. W. Norton, 1984.

Jennings, Francis, ed. *The History and Culture of Iroquois Diplomacy.* Syracuse: Syracuse University Press, 1995.

Kurath, Gertrude P. *Iroquois Music and Dance: Ceremonial Arts of Two Seneca Longhouses.* Smithsonian Institution, Bureau of American Ethnology, Bulletin 187. Washington, D.C.: U.S. Government Printing Office, 1964.

Levine, Mary Ann, Kenneth E. Sassaman, and Michael S. Nassaney, eds. *The Archaeological Northeast.* Westport, Conn.: Bergin and Garvey, 1999.

Mann, Barbara A., and Jerry L. Fields. "A Sign in the Sky Dating the League of the Haudenosaunee." www.wampum-chronicles.com/signinthesky.html.

Martin, Calvin. *Keepers of the Game: Indian-Animal Relationships and the Fur Trade.* Berkeley: University of California Press, 1978.

Mensforth, Robert P. "Human Trophy Taking in Eastern North America During the Archaic Period: The Relationship to Warfare and Social Complexity." In *The Taking and Displaying of Human Body Parts as Trophies by Amerindians,* edited by Richard J. Chacon and David Dye. New York: Springer, 2007.

Miroff, Laurie E., and Timothy D. Knapp. *Iroquoian Archaeology and Analytic Scale.* Knoxville: University of Tennessee Press, 2009.

Morgan, Lewis Henry. *League of the Iroquois.* New York: Corinth Books, 1962.

Mullen, Grant J., and Robert D. Hoppa. "Rogers Ossuary (AgHb-131): An Early Ontario Iroquois Burial Feature from Brantford Township." *Canadian Journal of Archaeology/ Journal Canadien dArcheologie* 16 (1992).

Parker, A. C. *Iroquois Uses of Maize and Other Food Plants.* Bulletin 144. Albany: New York State Museum, 1910.

Parker, Arthur C. *Seneca Myths and Folk Tales.* Lincoln: University of Nebraska, 1989.

Richter, Daniel. *The Ordeal of the Longhouse: The People of the Iroquois League in the Era of European Colonization.* Chapel Hill: University of North Carolina Press, 1992.

Snow, Dean. *The Archaeology of New England.* New York: Academic Press, 1980.

—.*The Iroquois.* Oxford: Blackwell, 1996.

Spittal, W. G. *Iroquois Women: An Anthology.* Ontario, Canada: Iroqrafts, 1990.

Talbot, Francis Xavier. *Saint Among the Hurons: The Life of Jean De Brebeuf.* New York: Harper and Brothers, 1949.

Tooker, Elizabeth, ed. *Iroquois Culture, History, and Prehistory.* Albany: The University of the State of New York, 1967.

Trigger, Bruce. *The Children of Aataentsic: A History of the Huron People to 1660.* Montreal: McGill-Queen's University Press, 1987.

Trigger, Bruce, ed. *Handbook of North American Indians, Vol. 15: Northeast.* Washington, D.C.: Smithsonian Institution Press, 1978.

Tuck, James A. *Onondaga Iroquois Prehistory: A Study in Settlement Archaeology.* New York: Syracuse University Press, 1971.

Wallace, Anthony F. C. *The Death and Rebirth of the Seneca.* New York: Vintage Books, 1972.

Walthall, John A., and Thomas E. Emerson, eds. *Calumet and Fleur-de-Lys: Archaeology of the Indian and French Contact in the Midcontinent.* Washington, D.C.: Smithsonian Institution Press, 1992.

Weer, Paul. *Preliminary Notes on the Iroquoian Family.* Prehistory Research Series. Indianapolis: Indiana Historical Society, 1937.

Whitehead, Ruth Holmes. *Stories from the Six Worlds: Micmac Legends.* Halifax: Nimbus Publishing, 1988.

Williamson, Ronald F., and Susan Pfeiffer. *Bones of the Ancestors: The Archaeology and Osteobiography of the Moat-field Ossuary.* Gatineau, Quebec: Canadian Museum of Civilization, 2003.

www.ingramcontent.com/pod-product-compliance
Lightning Source LLC
Chambersburg PA
CBHW011435240626
47153CB00011B/2998